*Strange Harmony*

*Strange Harmony*

To Nesta with much love
Alun

**ALUN JONES**

authorHOUSE®

*AuthorHouse™ UK Ltd.*
*1663 Liberty Drive*
*Bloomington, IN 47403 USA*
*www.authorhouse.co.uk*
*Phone: 0800.197.4150*

*© 2014 Alun Jones. All rights reserved.*

*No part of this book may be reproduced, stored in a retrieval system, or transmitted by any means without the written permission of the author.*

*Published by AuthorHouse    01/02/2014*

*ISBN: 978-1-4918-8889-6 (sc)*
*ISBN: 978-1-4918-8890-2 (e)*

*Any people depicted in stock imagery provided by Thinkstock are models, and such images are being used for illustrative purposes only.*
*Certain stock imagery © Thinkstock.*

*This book is printed on acid-free paper.*

*Because of the dynamic nature of the Internet, any web addresses or links contained in this book may have changed since publication and may no longer be valid. The views expressed in this work are solely those of the author and do not necessarily reflect the views of the publisher, and the publisher hereby disclaims any responsibility for them.*

# PREFACE

My soul, my soul,
There is a country far beyond the stars,
Where stands a winged sentry,
A sentry, all skilful in the wars:

There, above noise and danger,
Sweet peace sits crowned with smiles
And One, born in a manger
Commands the beauteous files.

He is thy gracious friend,
And O my soul awake!
Did in pure love descend
To die here for thy sake.

If thou canst get but thither,
There grows the flower of peace.
The rose that cannot wither,
Thy fortress, and they ease.

Leave then thy foolish ranges,
For none can thee secure
But One who never changes,
Thy God, thy life, thy cure.

*Henry Vaughan*
*1621-95*

# Chapter 1
# Final Rehearsal

The choir was half-way through 'the Hallelujah Chorus', when Mrs. Megan Roberts, leading contralto, dropped dead. Mr. Bryn Griffiths, conductor, lowered his flailing arms, a strange look of guilt and relief on his face. Mr. and Mrs. Roberts had been the only discordant notes in his three year association with the choir.

The choir stuttered to a halt. Miss Phoebe Jenkins the accompanist carried on for quite a few bars on her own, concentrating intently on her music. Then she looked round in embarrassment and alarm at the silent choir and the body. Phoebe, was also the village nurse, so she quickly bent down over Mrs. Roberts, felt for her pulse and announced quietly,

"She's gone."

Everyone started talking at once.

Dr. Handel Morgan's shrill tenor voice rose above the hubbub as he pushed his way unceremoniously through the choir members gathering around the body, his five foot four stature having as little effect on them as his professional skills had had,

"Out of the way everyone. Quick, let me try to resuscitate her!" He knelt beside the body.

"You keep your hands off her." The booming bass voice of Mr. Ray Roberts, husband of Megan and authoritarian choir treasurer, rang out as he stood protectively over his wife, white mane flowing above his towering frame.

This abrupt intervention stopped the doctor short:

"You never did her any good when she was alive, you're certainly not touching her now she's dead!" shouted Mr. Roberts, nearly out of control.

Everyone knew about the animosity between the doctor and Roberts. Handel had not diagnosed Megan's first heart attack after being called urgently from an important medical dinner, and arriving late to see his patient. Roberts had threatened to sue him and the doctor had responded rather unprofessionally by querying every last pound spent by the choir's treasurer thereafter.

The diminutive doctor now retorted, even more unprofessionally,

"Well, I'll have to sign the certificate, and the police might even ask me to do the Post Mortem as well, so I'll have to touch her won't I?".

Roberts responded with a loud snort of anger. He glared at the doctor then turned on the conductor,

*Strange Harmony*

"Bryn Griffiths. This is all your fault. The time you kept us practicing tonight was ridiculous. You did it deliberately, I know! Someone go and fetch Unwin the undertaker before we have another death on our hands."

Bryn took a step backwards in alarm at the treasurer's accusation, but Phoebe Jenkins, in an attempt to release the tension, sang out brightly

"I'll do it." Miss Phoebe had been accompanist for many years under the last conductor. She was tiny, ginger and freckled, and a competent, and sometimes quite inspiring, accompanist. The appointment of the new conductor had seemed to have given her a new lease of life.

Most of the choir had soon found out that Bryn had been inviting her to his bachelor flat in the High Street, ostensibly to explore and practice some of the new, trickier piano parts. Miss Phoebe clearly had been reinvigorated by these meetings.

The more straight-laced and prurient contraltos had openly suspected that other, more exciting explorations and more interesting skills than musical ones, were being practiced at these regular meetings, and their innuendos had recently become more and more unbridled and imaginative.

Phoebe returned, smiled at Bryn, and said,

"Mr. Unwin will be here in ten minutes." And turning to the recently bereaved treasurer, she added "He said don't worry, Mr. Roberts, he will see to everything."

Bryn relaxed a little. He had conducted many choirs and was well versed in the art of choir politics. Soon after his appointment, he had crossed swords with the now sadly deceased Mrs. Megan Roberts, who had been the Chairman of the choir since she and her husband had founded it over thirty years ago.

Mrs. Roberts, so he had found out, had not been in favour of his appointment. She had felt, correctly as it happened, that, unlike the last conductor, Bryn Griffiths wanted to have his own way with the choir and bring about changes to its well established programme of concerts for local charities. Bryn had confirmed that he wanted the choir to enter competitions, and had asserted that that was the best way to improve.

Choir competitions were anathema to Megan and Ray Roberts, and Bryn's kinds of improvements were certainly not on their agenda.

However, Bryn eventually had been appointed by the new Choir Committee, and had quickly become popular with most of the choir, for he was a very striking man: tall, dark, with long, black hair waving down the back of his neck. He thought it gave him an appropriate artistic presence; the Roberts' told all their friends it made him look ridiculous.

Most of the young sopranos, on the other hand, had found his commanding, and vigorous leadership attractive, and obviously for some of them, alluring.

Miss Phoebe, the middle-aged accompanist, was not the only one to enjoy special practices with Bryn. Soon after his appointment he had started inviting some of the members, mainly young sopranos, to his flat for extra rehearsals. It was all supposed to be very hush-hush, except that the sopranos involved had drawn up what they called 'the conductor's list', and jealously guarded any additions to it.

Bryn knew that Megan Roberts had found out about his list, and that she and her husband had started moves to get him dismissed on grounds of gross misconduct because of his supposed extra-musical activities with the ladies of the choir.

No wonder her sudden death aroused a mixture of emotions in him: the practice actually had been long and arduous, and he *had* known that Megan suffered from a serious heart condition. Now with her gone, much of the opposition to his intention to improve the choir might well dissolve . . . .

However, he had no time to dwell on that possibility, because the alarming speculations he heard all around him bubbling from the shocked choir, made him feel he should get some semblance of order back in the room. He suggested firmly,

"If Unwin is not going to be here for another ten minutes we'd all better sit back in our seats and calm down a little," then, attempting to lift the dark mood that had settled over the choir, he added

"Megan did a lot for this choir. Perhaps we could sing something quietly in her honour while we are waiting. How about Mozart's Ave Verum?"

"Hail! The conquering hero comes would be more appropriate!" This loaded intervention came from Karen Thomas, who ran the village café and grocery store. Karen had a sharp face, a sharp mind, and an even sharper tongue. Bryn had had early experience of the edge of her sharpness, so he had resolved to keep her off his list, and Karen had never really forgiven him for the exclusion.

Neither had she forgiven Megan and Ray Roberts for engineering a successful opposition to her planning application for an extension to her café. She now added nastily

"We should sing it very loudly as a warning to wherever she is going; and I bet I know where that is!" This remark shocked even the hardest hearts in the choir, but only one voiced piped up in protest:

"Oh that's not fair Karen. We all know Auntie Megan was a hard lady but there was nothing bad in her."

*Strange Harmony*

This defence of the Chairman came from Maggie Phillips, her niece, the youngest member of the choir, a very attractive fifteen year-old: tall, blonde and slim, with a figure developed beyond her years. She was vivacious and bubbly and had shocked the older women by flirting provocatively with any of the men who would encourage her. And very few had not.

"Nothing bad, my eye!" retorted Karen, "She could be positively venomous—if you'd heard what she'd said about *your* goings on with Bryn Griffiths, you would say so too." At this insinuation there was a sharp intake of breath around the choir.

Bryn immediately noticed that some of the younger sopranos were looking at Maggie in surprise. Maggie, red in the face, was just about to counter the allegation angrily, when Bryn, feeling that, as conductor, he had better halt Karen's slanderous attack commanded sternly,

"Now come on, let's stop all this nastiness, what with poor Megan still lying here . . . ."

At that moment the tension was fortunately broken by Unwin's trolley being pushed noisily through the door, Unwin himself, immediately behind it, reverential and a trifle obsequious, addressed the silent Mr. Roberts, who was sitting beside his wife in some distress now, apparently deaf to the slanderous comments about her character,

*Alun Jones*

"Oh. There's terrible Mr. Roberts, isn't it." Unwin commiserated in his calm, professional way, "Leave it all to me now. It'll be all right."

With that, there was an audible sigh of relief from the choir; Unwin, with some ceremony, put Mrs. Robert's body on his trolley and wheeled her out from the school room, accompanied by Mr. Roberts, head down and solemn.

As they got to the door, Bryn called out, "Wait a minute, Mr. Roberts, I'll come with you to see you're all right", and he joined the entourage as it started its journey down the corridor.

"Now that's what I call a lovely man, after all Ray Roberts has said about him" exclaimed Phoebe Jenkins, beaming with admiration after her conductor.

"That's what I call a guilty conscience" snarled Karen Thomas.

Suddenly they were interrupted by a loud wailing. It came from Maggie Phillips, apparently overcome by the emotion of seeing Mrs. Roberts wheeled out. She sobbed,

"Isn't it awful. I wonder who'll be next?"

The more superstitious contraltos shivered, assuming that she meant who would be the next member to expire in a Messiah practice! The younger, more easily aroused sopranos, however, thought that Maggie was just expressing her hope of being the next addition to the conductor's list, especially as Karen had just hinted that it could be more than possible.

Although he knew that Karen had got it wrong, Bryn suddenly began to look at Maggie in a new light when he noticed the young sopranos becoming more aware of the serious competition they might now be facing in the shape of this nubile young vision, who, through her ridiculously attractive tears, had posed the question.

As though to answer it herself, Maggie, quickly overcoming her consternation, ran after the entourage which had followed Megan's body out of the room, and called out brightly,

"Wait for me Bryn, I'll come with you, Mrs. Roberts was my auntie after all!"

Bryn looked around at her with a little quiver of excitement. The unfortunate demise of the choir's reactionary Chairman and leading contralto had suddenly opened the way for more than an easier introduction of new music for the choir, and a changed balance in its harmony!

# Chapter 2
# Safety First

The following morning Ray Roberts, much to his secretary's surprise, was in his office by his usual time of eight o'clock. She greeted him,

"Good morning Mr. Roberts. I really didn't expect you in this morning. I'm so sorry to hear about your wife. It must be awful to . . . ."

"Thanks, Jane. There's nothing I can do at home, so I thought I'd be better off here. It's not all that different to tell you the truth. Since her heart attack Megan has got into the habit of staying in bed until lunch time most days, so I never see her when I leave, anyway. Unwin is looking after most of the formalities for the funeral; I suppose I'll just carry on as usual."

With that he put his hand on his secretary's shoulder and brushed it slowly and softly across the back of her neck. She pulled away from him abruptly and said firmly,

"No, Mr. Roberts. No more we said, now didn't we? I really don't want to do it again. If my Bryan found out I would never forgive myself."

*Strange Harmony*

"O.K., Jane, O.K. But you know how I feel about you, and you *have* done very well out of your promotion . . ."

"Yes and I've earned that by sorting out the shambles your last secretary left you in. It's just got to stop now, I've told you, I can't risk anyone finding out."

"No one will find out. And in any case they wouldn't say anything. If they did. It would be more than their job's worth."

"And it would be more than *my* job's worth if Bryan found out. So that's it.

Now, as you are here, Mr. Haydn Morgan asked to see you again urgently. You've put him off at least twice this last week—he said it's about the new safety switches . . ."

"It would be. They haven't been ordered yet, so I really don't want to see him, but if you've fixed it we'd better get it over with."

"Well I told him you might be in, so he's coming round at ten. I'll get some tea ready for you."

Ray Roberts and Haydn Morgan had never hit it off. To start with Haydn was Dr. Handel Morgan's brother and sympathised with the antipathy the doctor had towards Roberts. But more seriously, Haydn had been appointed as mining engineer after the passing of the Coal Mines Act in 1911, only two years earlier.

The Act had eventually been passed in response to the frightening number of mining explosions reported around the country, and the ensuing public revulsion and Trades

Union representation that had markedly increased as a result of the appalling number of deaths of miners.

Many Accident Inquiries had revealed a serious lack of safety procedures employed by most mining companies. Analyses had provided more and more information about the causes of accidents and had shown that a complex set of circumstances contributed to many of the tragic incidents which had been reported.

Mine owners were well aware that combating all these causes would add considerable costs to the production of coal, so naturally there had been powerful resistance to any legislation to control safety in their mines.

However at the beginning of the century, the enormous increase in the volume of production of coal and the associated alarming number of deaths in the industry led the government to intervene and pass laws to control mine safety.

Haydn Morgan had been appointed to ensure that the new safety regulations for mines required by the 1911 Act were properly followed. In his new job it was inevitable that he would cross swords with Roberts who, as mine manager, was required by the owners to produce as much coal as they could sell, at the lowest possible cost.

The first two years of Haydn's appointment had been one continuous obstacle race. Every meeting with Roberts ended in heated argument and little agreement on the action needed to make the mine a safer place of work. But, this particular morning, Haydn was determined to convince Roberts about what was needed and thought that the death of the mine manager's own wife might make him a little more sensitive about the lives of his workers.

"Morning, Mr. Roberts," Haydn, greeted the manager solemnly when he entered Robert's office just after ten o'clock, "Sorry to hear about Megan; appropriate she went out singing, I suppose."

"Appropriate, my foot" Roberts retorted, "More like deliberate, I reckon Bryn Griffiths knew very well Megan was about to get him for professional misconduct for playing about with some of the girls in the choir. He had to do something about it pretty quickly. That practice was ridiculously long; but I'll get him, don't you worry."

"Well, getting down to brass tacks, now we're here, it's not Bryn Griffiths I'm worried about. It's the new safety switches."

"I'VE TOLD YOU. We ordered them eighteen months ago, soon after you came and made that ridiculous list of things we needed to do for the Act."

"And I've told you, *those* switches are all in and working, but we haven't even ordered the ones for the new No.4 and No.5 North seams yet. You know we're in contravention of the Act until they're in."

"And you know, because I've told you umpteen times, they were not in our budget. We'll have to wait until next year."

"They can't wait, Mr. Roberts. Look, I've written this report for Mr Crayton and the Board asking them to increase the safety budget. You can use that to get the money out of them. I know none of you are very keen to spend money on anything other than increasing production and profit, but . . . ."

"You watch your tongue, Morgan, or I'll have your job."

"I'm responsible to the Area Board, so my job's O.K. You just remember what happened five years ago. You all got away very lightly after that. It'll be a different matter if it happens again, God forbid."

"Are you threatening me?" Roberts was going red in the face now.

"No. Just warning you." Haydn recognised the signs of Robert's rising temper, and answered as gently as he could, "We've got to satisfy all the new requirements, and it's my job to see we do, so there's no point in keeping on quarrelling about it. And while we're at it, there's also not enough water laid on in No.4 and 5. The dust the men are having to work in is beyond all sense, and we've done nothing about getting the new fans for reversing the ventilation through the shafts either . . ."

Roberts exploded, "IT'S ONLY TWO YEARS SINCE THAT RIDICULOUS ACT. You can't expect us to do it all at once. We've got coal to produce."

"We've also got men's lives to protect . . . ."

"Don't give me all that nonsense. It's protecting their jobs the men'll thank us for, and we can only do that by staying profitable."

"I know we'll never agree on that, but it's not a matter of agreement now. It's a statutory requirement and there are rules we've got to keep to or we'll be liable."

"So you keep on telling me," Roberts answered, less heated now, "All right I'll order the new switches today, and I'll put the ventilation fans on the next Board agenda, will that satisfy you?"

"That's a good start, but I won't be satisfied until all the new safety equipment is in and working. Then we'll be O.K." Haydn was relieved that at least they had got some agreement to make progress on the safety front, but he knew he would still have to check that the orders for the remaining new switches had actually been sent off. He had learnt not to trust Robert's easy promises.

Roberts started to read some papers on his desk. "Right, if that's all, I've got to check all the arrangements for the opening of the railway line. The Board wants to make a big thing of it, Michael Clarkson, the M.P. is supposed to be coming, so all the press will be there. See you then." Haydn left the office abruptly.

# Chapter 3
# Post Mortem

About the same time that Roberts and his engineer were having their discussion, Mary Taylor was sitting with her regular lady friends around one of the gingham-clad, pine tables in Karen Thomas's pleasant little café. It was their usual gathering for mid-morning tea.

She looked around at her companions, leaned over the table, and whispered conspiratorially,

"Tell me, do you think Bryn Griffiths *really* did it deliberately?"

Karen moved in closer, pretending to tidy some of the other tables which were dotted around the little room. She had decorated it herself, brightly in creamy yellow to counteract the rather dark, heavily oak-beamed ceiling which, she felt, gave the room its attractive character. It had become a favourite meeting place for those select ladies of the village who had both time and money for such a luxury as morning tea. Karen's gorgeous, home-made cream cakes had soon contributed to the attraction of their meeting together.

The group was constituted almost entirely of wives of the mine managers and deputies. They all lived at the upper end of the village in detached houses with their own front gardens.

Karen knew that the wives of the miners and navvies, who lived in the terraced houses with their front doors opening directly onto the street at the lower end of the village, could never have afforded to *buy* their morning tea, even if they could have found time from their daily drudgery to stop for it.

She felt that, if the ladies of the upper village were willing to spend the money their husbands earned very easily compared with the miners and navvies they employed, she was only too ready to take it from them.

However, she found that serving tea and cakes also provided a very effective way of tapping into village gossip. She didn't want to miss any of *this* morning's topic of conversation, which clearly was going to be a post mortem on Megan's untimely death, so she moved as close to the table as she dared, to hear Mary Taylor continue her probing,

"I mean, he knew about her weak heart didn't he, and he certainly will find it easier to get his own way with the choir now with Megan gone . . ."

"You surely don't think he lengthened the practice hoping it might *kill* her?"

Betty Thomson was clearly shocked at Mary's implied allegation. She was a large lady, as untidy and dark and rotund as Mary was smart, blonde and petit. She went on,

"I know that Megan never liked the way he ran the choir, and disagreed with practically everything new he introduced, but I can't imagine for one moment that Bryn Griffiths is the kind of man that would go that far."

"Ray thinks he is, though, doesn't he?"

This intervention came from Jane Price, Megan's closest friend; a tall thin lady with a sharply critical outlook on life. She straightened her severe grey skirt, poured herself another cup of tea, reached over to take one of the largest cream cakes left on the plate in the middle of the table, then carried on, her gimlet eyes holding the group transfixed,

"We all know that Ray and Megan haven't been at all happy about Bryn Griffiths since he took over the choir, and Ray's a dangerous enemy to make, I can tell you. If he thinks Bryn made that practice difficult deliberately, there's no imagining what might happen."

"Oh, Ray's not like that, surely Jane, he's already asked the choir to sing at the funeral, hasn't he?" Betty was just trying to be positive; she followed Jane's lead and reached for another large cream cake, obviously feeling that her considerable frame needed it far more than Jane's sylph-like form did.

"That's the point," Jane retorted, through a mouthful of cake, "Bryn Griffiths is not coming to the funeral!"

"WHAT?" her friends exclaimed in unison.

"But he can't do that." Mary Taylor reacted immediately.

"Oh yes he can," went on Jane, pleased at the consternation her news had caused, "He told Phoebe that he's got some previous appointment in Cardiff and can't come. He's already written to Ray to apologise for missing the funeral."

"Ray will go berserk if the choir doesn't sing at Megan's funeral after all she's done for it." Mary nearly choked on her Madeira cake.

"Oh, we're going to sing all right," Jane replied, "Phoebe said she'll conduct us from the organ. Ray is keen for us to sing some Mozart in the funeral service. Look, ask her yourself, she knows all about it," she added, as she saw Phoebe come rushing into the café.

"I thought I'd find you here," said Phoebe breathlessly, looking around the table, "You're all coming to Megan's funeral aren't you?" There were nods of assent from all the ladies. "Good. Ray wants us to sing some Mozart in the service, so I'm rushing around checking that we're all going to be there."

"Of course we are—all except Mr. Bryn Griffiths, or so we hear." Jane replied, with a sharp edge to her voice. "What excuse is he giving?"

"He's got a chance of the associate organist's post in the cathedral and the auditions and interviews are on Monday. It is too good a chance for him to miss," answered Phoebe, loyally defending her conductor and friend.

"Hardly more important than Megan's funeral, I would have thought." Jane Taylor voiced what most of the group were thinking, tea and cakes forgotten for the moment. Her friends nodded their agreement.

"Now be fair, Jane." Phoebe responded. "Bryn doesn't owe Megan anything. You know it was she who blocked his application to the Education Committee to teach up at the senior school. She dug up the allegation about that girl in his last job that swung the vote against him."

Karen moved even closer, she knew exactly what Phoebe was talking about. Like most of the villagers, she had enjoyed the furore that had blown up over the appointment of the music teacher. A lot of very nasty innuendos about the applicants had flashed around the village. Bryn Griffiths and Ray Roberts, who was Chairman of the Committee assessing the applications at the time, had been at the centre of the row.

Phoebe, annoyed now, went on

"You couldn't expect Bryn to let Megan's funeral spoil his chance of the cathedral job, now could you, after all she and Ray have done to ruin his career since he came to us?"

*Strange Harmony*

"Well I think he ought to be there; he's the conductor, so he should conduct the choir at the funeral, especially as Megan was our founder chairman," said Jane firmly, expressing her own loyalties.

"Hear. Hear," came loudly from most of the group. Phoebe, tiny, ginger and now unusually belligerent, answered them with some spirit,

"Well he won't be there, and I'll be conducting. So there." With that she flounced out from the café.

"You can see whose side *she's* on," said Jane Price, a knowing smirk on her face. "Megan was probably quite right about what goes on in those meetings between our accompanist and our conductor. Practising new music my foot. Personally, I wouldn't put anything past him, and Phoebe is *very* suggestible. But I still think he should be at the funeral."

"How about another pot of tea, ladies. You must be thirsty after all that discussion." Karen Thomas approached the table openly now, attempting to dispel the heated atmosphere that had developed in the group; feeling it may not be good for business. She had not been surprised that the ladies all backed Megan and Ray. They had been members of the choir since it had been formed and had always taken sides with the Roberts couple against the changes their new conductor had initiated. Karen knew that the special practices for sopranos that he had introduced had particularly riled them.

"That'll be a good idea Karen thanks, replied Betty Thomson, settling herself firmly back in her chair, clearly relieved to get off the subject of the coming funeral. But Jane wasn't ready to let it go. She looked aggressively at Karen and said,

"Yes, get us another pot Karen. I've noticed you've been listening to everything we've said, so tell us what you think, you've been in the choir since it started."

She relished putting the café owner on the spot, but Karen quite enjoyed a bit of conflict too, so by the time she got back with the tea she had decided to say what she really thought, even though the group were her best customers and she might well upset them, so taking a deep breath, sh e said,

"Well, I can quite understand why Bryn is avoiding the funeral. Megan and Ray Roberts have always made things difficult for him, to say the least. After all they've said about him in the past, I think it would be almost hypocritical for him to be there."

"HYPOCRITICAL INDEED!" Jane Taylor exploded, as she stood up, glowering at Karen, her tall frame quivering from head to toe, "It is his *duty* to go!" she almost shouted, stamping her foot, in temper. "But I would have expected *you* to support him. You have never been on Megan Roberts' side. Or Ray's, for that matter, *and* we know why!" This latter remark she added with a knowing look at her companions, as she sat down again.

"I'm not taking sides," responded Karen, coolly, "I'm just saying I can understand Bryn's position. Shall I pour the tea?"

She knew exactly what Jane Price was alluding to, and she chose to ignore it. She was well aware that Jane, and pretty well all the other inhabitants of the village, knew that it was Ray Roberts who had influenced the Council to refuse her requests for a liquor license and permission to extend her café.

What Jane, or any of the other inhabitants of the village didn't know, was that Karen had a much more personal reason for not being on Ray Roberts' side.

## *Chapter 4*
# The Funeral

On the day of Megan Robert's funeral, quite early in the morning, a sad little family group gathered in the Roberts' large, pretentious house at the top end of the village. The garden, as usual, was immaculate, surrounding borders redolent with a wide variety of rose-bushes and shrubs, lawns cut as close as bowling greens, and flowers beginning to display splashes of colour in the morning sun.

In the middle of the beautifully furnished front room, which overlooked the curved, stone-edged driveway, stood a black-clad, rather portentous looking Ray Roberts, white winged shirt collar dutifully showing off his black cravat. Beside him, Megan's coffin, suitably expensive, waited on Unwin's trolley for the proceedings to begin. A little way behind it stood Evan Philips, Rays brother-in-law, and his daughter, Maggie, together with a line of black-coated men and women, all appropriately solemn cousins of the Roberts.

Near the door of the room stood Unwin and his wife, who always assisted him in his undertaking duties, dressed as they always were, in formal black garb.

*Strange Harmony*

The Reverend David Davies, Baptist minister, addressed them all in his impressive, deep bass voice, which Maggie always thought sounded like dark brown chocolate. He was black-gowned and dog-collared, a large, rotund and self-important man, almost as tall as Roberts himself, with horribly scarred and deformed ears, which, just like Robert's ears, effectively advertised the rugby scrimmaging days which they had shared when they were both much younger.

"Ray and friends." The Revd. Davies boomed. "It's good to be here together to honour the passing of Megan, and to remember and give thanks for her life with us all. We will miss her deeply, as we know you will, Ray, and as will all the village which she loved and served with such great devotion."

He took a deep breath and Evan Philips responded with a loud 'Here, here!' Maggie winced and thought that interjection was a bit inappropriate for the occasion, but then she realised that her Dad would not want to say 'Amen', as he was not a chapel man, like her Uncle Ray.

The minister was beginning to enjoy himself, as he was now in his favourite place at the centre of attention, but he forced himself to cut short his praise of Megan as he wanted to save all his most eloquent and colourful phrases for the big chapel service which was to follow.

After a few brief sentences, he brought the simple house service to an end with a prayer, to which all the mourners, including Evan, responded 'Amen'. With this dismissal, the Revd. walked out into the hall-way and invited them all to follow,

"Right then, friends, we'll go and join the others in the chapel now." And then he added rather formally, as he felt befitted the occasion,

"Mr. Unwin, will you lead the way please?"

This last request may have satisfied the Revd. Davies' sense of drama but it was, as it happened, unnecessary, for Unwin had already pushed the trolley and its coffin out through the door, and was on his way down the drive towards the waiting hearse. He and his wife, with expert ease, slid the coffin from the trolley into the flower-bedecked, four-wheeled vehicle, which they had converted for use as their hearse, and then went around to hold the heads of the shining black shire horses, which for years, had pulled it for those villagers who could afford such funereal luxuries.

The rest of the family formed up behind the hearse, Ray Roberts and the Revd. Davies at their head, and they proceeded slowly down to the Baptist chapel which stood hugely in the centre of the village.

The severe, upright, wooden pews of the chapel were filled with six hundred or so black-garbed, solemn people, all the ladies wearing black hats of strikingly similar shape and size. The wearers may have been non-conformist in their religion, but were obviously orthodox in their choice of head-gear.

The front pews were reserved for the local dignitaries, or 'the crachach' as the ordinary village people would ungraciously, and somewhat disparagingly, call them. So the local Member of Parliament, the Chairman of the County Council, the Chairman of the Parish Council and their wives sat importantly together towards the front, registering both their own standing and, by their presence, that of Ray and Megan Roberts.

Immediately behind them sat the mine owners and their wives and a sprinkling of other important people of the area, all of them looking a little uncomfortable in the starkly non-conformist chapel surroundings, the normal place of *their* attendance on God being the Cathedral in the city some miles town the main road of the valley.

Ray would have preferred the funeral to have been there, but after he was promoted to the Board of the mine, whenever he had suggested that Megan and he might benefit socially and economically from joining the owners and other community leaders in the Cathedral, she had refused, preferring to remain resolutely loyal to their up-bringing in the Baptist chapel and to the strict non-conformism of their forebears.

She would have considered, far more than Ray would have done, that changing their religious allegiance would have constituted an insult to their parents, whose ambition and sacrifice alone had enabled them both to go to University and arrive at the social standing they now enjoyed.

So it was that Ray found himself leading her funeral cortege into the familiar sights and sounds of their village Baptist chapel, which was buzzing with the anticipation of 'a really big funeral'

The powerful, sombre sounds of the organ greeted them as they reached the chapel. Miss Pheobe was playing it as usual, double forte for the occasion, surprisingly out of character for her slight frame. She had been organist at the chapel since she was a teenager and had learnt to overcome her natural shyness by producing a volume of sound that exuded confidence. One result of this was to encourage the singers in the congregation to produce an equally magnificent sound.

This they were doing as Megan was carried down the left hand aisle to the space in front of the pulpit where the deacons sat in their 'big seats', each of them proudly wearing a gold watch chain across the black waistcoats that their ample stomachs filled roundly.

The singing was being led enthusiastically by the choir, who were arranged around the gallery, facing the pulpit and organ. These two impressive edifices served to demonstrate to all, the traditional twin cores of the chapel's non-conformist approach to worship:

*Strange Harmony*

preaching and singing, which often, inappropriately, vied with each other for supremacy.

Ray had asked them to sing Megan's favourite hymn as her coffin entered the chapel and joined the waiting mourners. They sang loudly in four part harmony as usual, and in Welsh, which had not been usual for some years, but which now was being used to acknowledge the language of the chapel's two-hundred years' religious history in the valley, and of Megan's own upbringing. Following their tradition they repeated even more loudly, the last chorus: 'Bendithia fi, fy Ngheidwad, bendithia nawr. O bless me now my Saviour, I come to thee,' and then they all sat down.

The singing raised the emotional level of the gathering considerably, which suited the Revd. David Davies well, as he climbed the steps of the enormous, decorative pulpit, its curved, dark oak banisters sealing it off from the congregation and, at the same time, providing an impressive theatrical support for his performance.

He welcomed the Member of Parliament, the Chairmen of Councils, and the other dignitaries fulsomely, and acknowledged the presence of the other mourners rather perfunctorily in his opening remarks, before launching out on his long introduction to the service.

He then embarked on a detailed history of Megan's life, starting with the move her parents had made from the slate quarries of North Wales to the booming attraction of the coal fields in the South Wales valleys. He continued expansively with the success of her schooldays, which many of their contemporaries in the attentive congregation had shared, onto her time at University with Ray, which luxury very few of them had been able to afford.

After detailing all the things Megan had done for the local community, including the launching of both the Friends of the Hospital and the village choir with her husband, he concluded his eulogy with,

"So, friends, we give thanks for the life of Megan Roberts, one of the most well loved and respected leaders of our community. May she rest in peace."

There was a murmur of approval from around the congregation, interspersed with a few 'Amens' as Revd. Davies strode grandly from the pulpit to be replaced by the Chairman of the County Council. Ray had been on the Council ever since he was promoted to be manager of the mine on which virtually the whole village depended for employment and livelihood, so it was natural that the Chairman would support him at his wife's funeral.

The Chairman, fortunately for the listening congregation, was quite brief in expressing his thanks for, and admiration of Megan's contribution to civic affairs over the years, but this was followed by a long and boring eulogy by the Head Master of the local school of which, even though they had no children of their own, Megan and Ray, at different times, had been Governors.

Then came the time for the choir to make their contribution. As Miss Pheobe returned to the organ stool to accompany them, she reflected on the adulation the Roberts' had been regaled with by all these important members of the community. She couldn't help thinking 'And these are the two people that Bryn Griffiths has not only drastically offended by taking over their choir, but now has snubbed by going to an appointment in Cardiff rather than attending Megan's funeral and leading the choir in her honour.'

She glanced at Ray's face in her organ mirror and blanched as she recognised fury written all over it. 'There's going to be trouble.' She thought, feeling anxious about Bryn's future in the choir and the village, however the choir was standing, waiting expectantly for her to lead them in 'Myfanwy', another of Megan's favourite pieces, from the organ.

She began the introduction quietly and the choir started perfectly together. They knew the song so well they didn't really need a conductor: as their leading tenor often said, 'They could sing it backwards.' But that wasn't the issue about Bryn's absence. It was the fact that he had rated anything more important than attending the funeral, especially as Megan was the choir's founder chairman, as well as being Ray's wife. The resulting feeling of humiliation and affront fired Ray Roberts' anger insanely.

The choir finished the stirring harmonies of the piece singing double piano, and there was hardly a dry eye in the chapel. 'Myfanwy' invariably had that effect on Welsh congregations, apart from all the personal emotions of this special occasion.

Revd. Davies announced the last hymn: 'Abide with me', another of Megan's favourites, this time sung in English, in which the members of the congregation were able to give vent to their highly-charged emotions by singing loudly and with great fervour. As many of them commented to their neighbours 'Megan would have been pleased.'

Unwin and the other coffin bearers came to the front to carry Megan out and Revd. Davies said a blessing over the coffin and the congregation.

It took quite a time for all the people to file out of the chapel and for the men to form up in line behind the magnificently be-decked hearse, with its two shire horses waiting patiently to lead them up the hill to the cemetery.

The women, as was the tradition, did not go to the cemetery but walked up the road to Megan and Ray's house to prepare the funeral meal for their close friends, which would conclude the proceedings after the men returned.

The funeral procession started to wend its way from the chapel to the cemetery, the miners who were off-shift at the time, dutifully and sensibly attending the funeral of their manager's wife, eyed the shire horses with admiration and relief. If the funeral had been for one of their own friends they would have been toiling up the hill carrying the coffin on foot.

Megan's position in the community, however, earned her the luxury of being taken up to the cemetery on Unwin's best hearse. It was an impressive last journey, a long line of black-suited men walking sombrely behind Ray and the Revd. Davies, some of them singing Welsh funeral hymns quietly to themselves.

At the end of the short committal service around the grave, the mountain air was filled with the rich sounds of a hundred or so men's voices blending in harmony, singing one of their favourite funeral hymns: 'Rho im yr hedd . . . Give me the peace which passes understanding.'

As they dispersed to walk back down the mountain to the village, Evan Philips moved alongside his brother-in-law and said quietly

"That was a wonderful funeral, Ray. Megan would have enjoyed that."

"What! With the choir having to sing without their conductor?" Ray's face was usually abnormally florid, but now it looked like thunder. "Bryn Griffiths has done many stupid things in his time with us, but missing the funeral is one step too far." Ray's voice shook with fury. Evan tried to calm him,

"Well you said you could get him dismissed from the choir because of all that business with the sopranos . . ."

"I'll do that all right, but that's not nearly enough now. I can do much more than that to him." Evan feared his brother-in-law might have a heart attack right there at his wife's funeral.

"But Ray . . . ." He started. Ray interrupted him.

"I've got an idea that'll sink him properly, and your Maggie is part of it. You know he's started having her back to his place for so-called singing lessons on her own, even though she's under-age."

"Fair play now. He's giving her the lessons for free."

"For free, my foot. She's paying for them don't you worry. And not with money. He's done it before with girls in his last school."

"WHAT?"

"He got away with it then, but we can cook up some evidence easily, and I've got enough pull with the Bench to get it to stick this time. A few years in prison will teach him not to take me on again."

"You don't mean he's trying it on with Maggie too." Evan was clearly shocked at the allegation.

"Of course he is."

"I'LL KILL HIM." Evan's fury matched Ray's now.

"Good. That sounds even better." Ray became icy cold at the thought of an alliance with his brother-in-law. "We'll fix him properly this time. But we'll need to think it through."

# *Chapter 5*
# The Funeral Party

While the men followed Megan's coffin up to the cemetery, Megan's special lady friends gathered in her house to prepare the funeral party for the select group of people who had been invited. Jane Price, Megan's closest friend, and one of the leading society ladies, was organising the whole affair with her usual severe efficiency.

She had arranged for Karen Thomas to provide most of the food from her café, but a small number of the ladies, whose cakes were known to be reasonably edible, had also cooked cakes especially for the event.

Naturally, all the usual morning tea group were there. Mary Taylor, smartly turned out as always, but in black to mark the occasion, started off the conversation,

"It was a lovely service, wasn't it? I thought the choir did very well without Bryn, didn't you?"

"Yes I did. But Ray wasn't at all happy about it, was he?" Jane replied, showing the others how she wanted the cakes laid out.

"Wasn't happy? He was absolutely LIVID." Betty Thomson joined in the discussion and relaxed her large,

*Alun Jones*

untidy frame in the most comfortable easy-chair in the room, for she wasn't going to be bossed around by Jane Price.

"Well what did you expect, Bryn Griffiths was positively insulting, not coming to the funeral," said Jane, ignoring the fact that Betty had opted out from arranging the plates of cakes, and doing it herself.

"He did have that interview in the Cathedral though, didn't he?" Said Mary, trying hard to be unbiased, but assiduously doing what Jane had told her.

"THAT won't do him any good,." answered Jane sharply, "Ray's very friendly with the Bishop, so Bryn will never get the job."

Mary pretended to look shocked, "Surely Ray wouldn't use his influence in that way?"

"Oh yes he will." Jane retorted. "Bryn has managed to cross him ever since he came to the choir. Now he's just gone too far. Ray will be out for his blood from here on." Jane knew exactly how angry Ray felt about Bryn.

"Well I still think it was a nice service," Said Mary looking hungrily at the food,

"And this is a lovely lot of food Karen has sent. Have we *got* to wait until the men come back?"

"Yes we have," said Jane, re-establishing her role as leader, "We can't start until Ray is here. They won't be long now."

"Good. They can't come soon enough for me." Exclaimed Mary, who then launched archly into her

*Strange Harmony*

favourite topic of village gossip, "Tell me, do you happen to know what Maggie Philips did after she followed Bryn and Ray out of the practice after Megan died?"

Betty sat up in her chair, suddenly stimulated by the possibility of some interesting village gossip, and volunteered,

"I heard they all went to Unwin's, he phoned the hospital and the police, just in case they wanted to investigate the death, even though we all saw what happened and Megan had a history of heart trouble."

This aroused Jane's interest, for she usually knew everything that was going on in the village and now needed to regain her position, so she added,

"Then Bryn and Maggie went back to his house, or so I heard, and she's been there before, supposedly for singing lessons."

Mary put on a look of mild shock, and continued her questioning,

"But she's only fifteen. They shouldn't be in his flat on their own, should they? ANYTHING could happen!"

"And probably does! "Answered Jane. "She's a very precocious young lady, AND she's very attractive and acts much too old for her age."

"Since her mother died she's become very head-strong, so her father told me," Betty added, needing to maintain her share of the discussion and at the same time wanting to re-align herself with Jane.

Mary, maintained her air of innocence, and retorted quietly,

"But he wouldn't risk it with a young girl like Maggie, would he?"

Jane answered conspiratorially,

"He's done it before, so Megan told me. She found out something from his last teaching job when he applied to teach here in the village . . . ."

Mary always liked to appear fair-minded, so she countered Jane's insinuation quickly,

"Oh, now, fair play Jane. That was shown to be a story made up by a girl in the school."

"No smoke without fire, I always say." Jane added, a rather unpleasant look on her face.

The ladies group quickly stopped their prurient conversation about Maggie and Bryn as they saw the men come walking up the drive, Ray alongside the Chairman of the Council and the Revd. David Davies next to them.

"Come on in gentlemen, we've got the kettle on, or perhaps you'd like something stronger." Said Jane in welcome, then her face fell as she noticed that the M.P. was not with the men. She asked them

"Where's Mr. Clarkson? He didn't come back with you?"

"No, Jane," Ray Roberts replied, as all the men helped themselves to the beer and spirits lined up on the table, "He had to go back to London for an important vote in the House. We were lucky he could come at all."

"Oh, that's a shame. I wanted to see him about the weekend arrangements."

Betty butted in anxiously,

"He will be coming to the opening of the railway on Saturday, won't he?"

She was referring to other big event of the week when the new railway was to be opened by Michael Clarkson, the local M.P. The mine owners had financed the building of the railway line to transport the ever increasing volume of coal they were producing, down the valley to the iron works, which they also part-owned, and to the port that now exported their coal all over the world. The line would increase their fortunes considerably.

"Oh he'll be there all right," Roberts retorted, "So we'll get all the police we asked for. That farmer's group means trouble."

The local hill sheep farmers and vegetable growers had lost out to purchase orders which had been served on the parts of their land that the new railway line would go through. In some cases farms had been split in two by the new track, leaving them unviable or at best, very difficult to operate.

The farmers felt they had been forced into unfair deals for their rented land and were incensed because they knew that the mine owners, and Roberts in particular, had been hand-in-glove with the local planners on the Council, so they had formed a protest group. The group had threatened to disrupt the opening ceremony and to protest to their Member of Parliament about the unfairness of the land deals, so Roberts had arranged with the Chief Constable for extra police to attend to control any trouble that might arise, and to keep the protestors well away from the M.P.

"Don't worry, Ray, there'll be no trouble," responded Evan Philips, who Ray and the owners had promoted from mine deputy to be the new manager of the railway line, "I've already seen the Police Inspector who'll be on duty and warned him there may be a violent protest. He knows exactly what to expect, and his men do, they've handled riots all round South Wales. They'll stand no nonsense."

"Good. I'm glad to hear it, Evan," replied Roberts, "It's best to be one step ahead of them. Now lead me to this food. Thanks ladies. It all looks very good."

With that the whole party, who now appeared to be more interested in the coming opening of the railway line than in poor Megan's demise, which after all, was the reason for their gathering together, tucked into the feast laid out before them.

# Chapter 6
# The Opening Of The Railway

The small group of angry, rather desperate men looked balefully across the line of uniformed policemen at the preparations for the official opening of the new rail-track. They were the farmers and small-holders through whose land the track had been laid for the twenty or so miles down to the coast, dividing up their farms and threatening their livelihood. With them could be seen a few miners who felt strongly enough to support their cause, for it hadn't helped that most of the navvies who had been employed to cut up the countryside and lay the track, had been brought over from Ireland.

The indignities and insults that had hurt most, however, had been the compulsory purchase orders passed by the local Councillors and planners, which had offered the small farmers such very poor deals for the land they had rented.

They knew full well that it had been the mine-owners who had influenced the Councils to force the orders through, and it was those very owners who would now make further fortunes through transporting their coal on their own railway line.

Even worse, some of the farmers and small landowners had supplied the horses and wagons which the owners had used to transport their coal since the mine was opened, and now they had lost even that income, because their wagons had been made redundant by the introduction of the railway.

It was not surprising, therefore,. that the twenty or so men whose livelihoods had been so drastically affected by the new railway were intent on disrupting its opening to make a public protest about the unfair way they had been treated.

The dark mood amongst them contrasted starkly with the celebrations that were going on at the new terminal for the railway which had been conveniently sited a short distance from the pit-head.

Crowds were beginning to gather from all over the area, for this was the most important event since the opening of the mine itself, about twenty years earlier. The usually drab, coal-dusted surroundings were ablaze with colour. Flags and flowers were everywhere, and the women, at least the younger ones, had discarded their usual black or brown dresses and aprons for bright party frocks: yellows, reds, and blues surprising the dark, iron wheels and cages which stood astride the pit shaft, and which kept on working whatever went on around them, taking men down into the earth for their daily labour and returning with the coal on which the economy of the area depended.

The mine owners had promised that the valley would become even more prosperous through the railway, so this was a day of rejoicing.

The stirring sounds of the local brass-band raised the crowd's anticipation as they came marching up the road from the village, leading the impressive column of dignitaries, who jealously guarded the political and financial power of the area.

At its head strode Michael Clarkson, the Member of Parliament, now back from London, eager to perform in front of the people who had elected him. As he passed, he waved and smiled at the crowds that thronged the roadway. The Chairmen, and most of the members of the various layers of local Councils followed close behind their M.P., the size of the chains around their necks striving to demonstrate the hierarchy of their importance.

Bringing up the rear of the entourage were the Chairman of the Board of Directors of the mine, and the other owners on the Board, their motives for celebrating being more financial than political, as they contemplated the considerable increase their bank balances would show as a result of the new rail facility.

Alongside them proudly strode Ray Roberts and Evan Philips, newly promoted to the Board of the Railway Company to join the mine owners in the new enterprise, and, like the owners, smiling broadly at the extent to which they too would benefit financially.

At the other end of the scale were the cheering miners and their families, for they had also benefited, albeit in relatively miniscule ways: the Trade Union had been demanding an increase in the miners' wages for some time after they had discovered how much the price of coal had increased on the export markets the previous year.

Wages were normally determined by the price the coal could be sold for, but the owners had resisted this particular demand for many months, specifically to time any rise in wages to coincide with the opening of the railway. Their careful planning had now paid off, because the miners and their families were this week, a few pence better off, and this, to them a significant benefit to their households, had improved their mood, and thus their reaction to the introduction of the railway. Had they known the actual size of the considerable reduction in the costs of production the rail link would be likely to contribute, and the fact that the owners were very unlikely to pass any of those benefits on to their workers, they would probably have cheered less loudly or maybe even have joined in protesting with their farmer neighbours.

. The brass band finished the march they had been playing with a flourish, the cheering, chattering crowd became silent and the opening ceremony was ready to begin. All the dignitaries arranged themselves noisily around the long table that had been set up outside the new terminal building, following their usual strict protocol.

Suddenly, from the waiting group of protestors, Huw Thomas, Karen's father, who had probably lost more than most of his fellow farmers and was obviously their leader gave a shout

"Right lads. Let's do it!"

With a great shout, the angry group of men broke through the line of policemen and ran through the crowd to the long table. Then with cries of

"We want justice!" and "Fair play for the farmers", they turned it over, spilling the flower arrangements and the jugs of water onto the ground. The crowd stared at the chaos in horror. The dignitaries cowered behind the upturned table in alarm.

Ray Roberts shouted to the policemen who were running after the protestors, lashing out at them furiously with their truncheons.

"Charge them with rioting!" He and Evan Philips, both large men and well able to look after themselves, tackled the excited men who were trying to approach the M.P. Around them police and protestors were fighting furiously, fists and boots and truncheons causing considerable damage.

The white table cloth that had emphasised the importance of the top table, was now strewn over the floor, spattered in blood.

The crowd looked at the melee with alarm and consternation, not really knowing which side to join. Then Ray's voice rang out above the shouting once more

"Here, Inspector, we've got the ring-leader. Handcuffs. Quickly!"

Ray and Evan had pinned Huw Thomas to the ground in front of the M.P.

"Prison for this one, and for any of the others you can catch." Snarled Ray, looking up pointedly at the Chairman of the County Council and helping the Inspector handcuff Huw.

The policemen considerably out-numbered the protestors and quickly gained the upper hand. When the rest of the farmer's group saw the capture of their leader, as many of them as were able tore themselves free, ran off up the valley, hotly pursued by truncheon-waving policemen.

As the police Inspector and some of his men marched Huw Thomas and a few other farmers from the group back to the village, Ray turned to an obviously frightened Michael Clarkson and said,

"We're sorry about that, sir. Just a few hot-heads I am afraid. They'll be caught and punished, don't you worry." And then, addressing some of the other dignitaries, he added with a confident authority going back to his rugby days,

"Now, if some of you gentlemen will help me put the table back, we can get on with opening the rail—track."

With that, appropriately on cue, the engine they had ordered especially from Germany, came chugging up the siding below the terminal, bathing both itself, and the crowds of people around it, in steam. Someone started cheering, and this encouraged the rest of the crowd to join in the welcome. Most of them had never seen anything like this great, steel, steaming beast that had at last appeared before them. Fortunately it served immediately to release the tension of the earlier fracas.

A symbolic blue ribbon was tied between the locomotive and the top table, the M.P. gave a humorous but somewhat attenuated speech, as he was still shaking from his recent experience of community action, the band struck up a martial fanfare which steadied him a little, and the ribbon was cut with great ceremony.

The engine let out a joyous 'hoot', and a great cloud of steam, and proceeded slowly down the siding towards the twelve trucks, full to their brims with coal, which were waiting to be hauled down to the port on their brand new tracks.

The crowd cheered enthusiastically but were soon quietened by a series of dreary, sometimes inarticulate, speeches by the important Chairmen and leaders of the Councils, all of whom had to say something but did not, in all cases, have something to say.

The formal speeches were then concluded by the Chairman of the Mining Board succinctly emphasising the economic advantages the mine, and now the railway, were bringing to all the inhabitants of the valley. The inhabitants, on their part, were lost to his special pleading, as they still felt quite good about the rises they had been given.

Ray Roberts then called on the choir to complete the celebrations with a rousing item and the National Anthem, totally ignoring the fact that, unlike the occasion of his wife's funeral, this time Bryn Griffiths was present to conduct the choir.

However Ray confirmed his antipathy towards the conductor by remaining seated at the top table and, with firmly folded arms, glaring balefully at Bryn, rather than taking up his usual place at the head of the bass section of the choir and obediently following the conductor's lead.

The top table dignitaries then began to disperse towards the tables of food that had been prepared especially for them, while the crowd gravitated towards the

*Strange Harmony*

tables where the owners had set up a limited amount of free ale in an attempt to create an impression of generosity. The miners were clearly not fooled by this gesture that was not at all in line with the usual attitude they noticed in their bosses, but nevertheless, they quickly took advantage of it.

Mary Taylor and the other lady-wives had organised the food, and had paid Karen Thomas to supply most of it. But this didn't stop Karen from becoming beside herself at the way her father had been treated. They hadn't been all that close since Karen had had her illegitimate son fourteen years ago, but she could still understand how he felt at the loss of his farm. It was as much as Karen's immediate friends had been able to do to stop her from joining him in the fight the protest had de-generated into.

She had told them that she had warned him not to go too far, but knew he wouldn't listen to her. She turned to Maggie Philips and the other friends who had helped to restrain her,

"Thanks all of you. It wouldn't have made any difference if I had piled in too. It would just have lost me my business as well as Dad's. He's finished if he ends up in prison. And it's just like Ray Roberts to see to that. I HATE HIM."

Maggie answered her sympathetically,

"We're all very sorry Karen. Even though my Dad's ended up running the railway, I still think it wasn't fair the way they dealt with the farmers. There's going to be a lot more trouble." Karen gave her a worried look, and replied,

"You can say that again. Dad and the other farmers won't let it go at just today's protest. There's going to be civil war in the valley because of what 's been done to them, and Ray Roberts and your Dad will be at the centre of it."

# Chapter 7
# Maggie Discovers Herself'

Maggie sang quietly to herself as she cleaned the brass in Ray Robert's big, attractive kitchen. She enjoyed being in the house, so large compared with her own, and she'd found that keeping it clean was not very arduous. After her Auntie Megan died, she had felt sorry for her Uncle Ray, so she had offered to come every week to do some cleaning for him, even though they had never had a great deal of contact while she had been growing up, and she had never found him very approachable or interested in her school progress or anything like that.

Granted he and Auntie Megan had always given her token birthday presents, and they *had* asked her to join their choir, but that was about as far as it had got. However, over these recent weeks she had got to know him a bit better and had discovered that she quite liked him: she'd even got used to his gruff, kind of bad-tempered way of speaking, and just assumed he talked like that to the miners in the colliery. Anyway it went with his size, and with the funny little frown he always seemed to have on his face.

He'd be home from the mine at about six: Maggie would have a cup of tea ready for him and they would sit and have a chat for a short while. She never grudged him the time the chatting took, for he paid her quite well for her work, and she knew that he was feeling very lonely now in the big house on his own. She had begun to feel that it was the least she could do for him.

She finished cleaning the brass, admired the shine she had put on it and replaced it proudly in the big glass-fronted cupboard in the parlour. She then skipped happily upstairs to tidy up Ray's bedroom and change the sheets, one of her regular chores.

She entered the big airy room, which was decorated beautifully in a restful, pale green. She bent down to smooth out the white, newly ironed sheets, and arranged the green bed-spread over the whole bed, noticing again with approval how well it matched the curtains. Typical of the 'posh' end of the village, she thought, as she remembered her own bed-spread which her mum had crocheted before the tuberculosis had killed her three years previously.

Maggie gave a sigh, she still missed her mum awfully; her dad always seemed a bit distant and they never talked very much. She supposed he was lonely too, really, so she felt she knew how her Uncle Ray felt.

She looked at the bed longingly, with its mattress, thick and soft and made with feathers, not at all like her own, which was the more usual hard, horse-hair mattress, to be found in most of the bedrooms of the valley. She wondered what it would be like to lie on a bed of feathers, so she slipped her shoes off and lay down, sumptuously, on the bed.

She thought to herself 'How beautiful. This is how the Queen must feel.' She lay back and luxuriated in the new feeling of opulence for a while. Then she surprised herself that, just lying there seemed to excite her young, burgeoning sexuality. A strong, healthy fifteen-year old, she had found for some time now, that she was beginning to enjoy day-dreaming, and even fantasising, about some of the boys at school.

Quite recently a boy, just a year older, had moved to the village with his family. They had come from Italy to open an ice-cream parlour because a number of their Italian friends and relatives had emigrated to the valleys of South Wales and had prospered as they found work in the booming factories and mines that coal and steel had multiplied. She had noticed that the Italian boy was much darker and taller than the Welsh boys she was used to, and she found herself very attracted, and yes, she had to admit to herself, excited, by his smouldering, sultry look and his black, almond eyes.

Lying back on the gorgeous bed, she closes her eyes and lets her imagination run away with her: Giovanni is standing at the bedroom door, looking at her with his wonderfully seductive eyes. She smiles at him and smoothes down the silky night-gown she is wearing. She can imagine what it is like quite clearly, as she has longed to wear one just like it ever since seeing it advertised in a glossy magazine of her Auntie's, all pale cream and alluring.

Giovanni leaves the door-way and moves silently and languidly towards her, looking straight into her eyes: she sinks down into the soft bed with a little quiver of delicious anticipation running thorough her young body, and looks up at him with, what she feels certain to be, inviting, welcoming eyes. She lets out a soft, murmuring sigh, unsteady with induced amorous excitement.

Suddenly her pleasant reverie was abruptly interrupted as the door was opened, not by Giovanni, but by her Uncle Ray, who stood, filling the door-way with his large frame, looking right at her: he said with a smile,

"Ah-ha, young Maggie. Caught you sleeping on the job, have we?"

Maggie sat up on the bed immediately, surprised, but not really alarmed, as her Uncle did not appear cross in anyway, although she did register that she hadn't seen him look at her in quite that way before.

*Strange Harmony*

"I'm sorry, Uncle Ray. You're early! I'd finished everything, so as I felt a bit tired and the bed looked so inviting I . . ."

"That's all right, Maggie," Ray interrupted her quickly, and came across the room to her. "I didn't mean it. You look just right on the bed actually. Lovely, in fact. Comfortable, is it?"

"Oh, yes. It's beautiful."

"It's even nicer inside the sheets." Ray added quietly.

"But I wouldn't go *in* the bed, Uncle Ray. I wouldn't dare. Anyway, I've only just changed the sheets."

"Well, feel free to get in anytime. You're becoming a very attractive girl, you know that, don't you?" He reached out to stroke her hair.

"Some of the boys at school seem to think so." She answered with a nervous smile, and moved away from him on the bed. "But I know what they're after, and I'm not ready for that yet."

She looked at her Uncle a little warily, and began to get off the bed.

"No, don't get off. Let me get you a drink," said Ray quickly.

"I'll go and make the tea," answered Maggie, just as quickly, and started to stand up.

"You just stay there and I'll get us something nicer than tea," Ray replied, gently pushing back on the bed, still with an encouraging smile on his somewhat florid face. He moved to the cupboard at the side of the bed,

"I always keep an extra night-cap in here in case I wake up and can't get to sleep again. Here, just try that, my girl. I guarantee it'll make you feel good."

With that, he poured two stiff gins, passed one to Maggie, and sat on the bed with her.

"What's this? I don't think I should . . . ."

"It's just a spot of gin. You've got to start sometime. Go ahead, just taste it."

Maggie had always been an adventurous, head-strong girl, but now she hesitated, remembering some of the stories her mother had told her about the ways of men.

"Go on, Maggie. Trust me. I wouldn't give you anything that was bad for you. Take a swig and role it round your tongue. It's great."

With this encouragement Maggie lifted up the glass and took a mouthful of the drink. The taste was new to her, and it stung her mouth just a little, but she felt it was by no means unpleasant. She swallowed the mouthful in one go.

"OOH!" She squealed, "It's hot all the way down to my tummy."

"There, I said it would do you good, didn't I? Try some more."

*Strange Harmony*

"It's quite nice, really," Maggie took another mouthful with some relish and leant back again on the pillows, feeling more relaxed.

"That's right, make yourself comfortable. Tell me. What would you like for your birthday. I know Megan and I have always given you kid's things. I really ought to get you something more grown-up this year. What would you *really* like" Ray smiled at her encouragingly and moved up the bed nearer to the girl.

Maggie's eyes lit up, seeing a possibility,

"What I want most is that dress they've got in Jones' the Drapers window. It's white with red flowers on it—but it's much too expensive for me. I'll never be able to afford that sort of thing."

"You play your cards right, my girl, and you'll be able to afford much more than that dress. But if that's what you want now, you shall have it."

"Gee. Thanks Uncle Ray that would be wonderful."

"You can drop the Uncle too, we're both old enough to be friends now. We ought to get to know each other better. Tell me, have you got a regular boy friend at school?" The girl hesitated. Ray moved closer still "Go on, I can keep secrets."

"No. Not regular. I'm friends with them all I suppose."

"I bet they try it on with you all the time. You'd be difficult for them to resist with a figure like you've got, I should think. Do you encourage them ever? Just a little bit, maybe?"

"Well, I suppose I like flirting with them. But that's all there is in it. They all know where they stand with me: I think some of the other girls let them go much too far."

"Aren't *you* tempted to go a bit further sometimes? Just to see what it's like?"

With that, Ray moved right up to the girl and put his hand on her leg. His hand was big, and Maggie could feel the warmth of it through the rough, woven fabric of her skirt. For just a brief moment, excited, she indulged herself in imagining it was Giovanni's hand and that she could feel it's warmth through the silk of the night-gown, but the memory of her mother's guiding words swiftly gained the upper hand, and she removed Ray's hand firmly from her leg, and got off the bed.

"I'd better go, now, Uncle Ray," she said, feeling just a little unsteady on her feet, and walked determinedly to the door. She found the door locked and looked back in alarm to see that Ray had caught up with her and was standing next to her, towering over her.

"You don't need to be frightened, Maggie," he said, seeing her consternation, "Here's the key. What'll you give me for it?" He smiled at her, "A quick kiss will do for now."

"Oh. That's easy, Uncle Ray." She answered, noting the 'for now', but, chose to ignore the potential danger in the situation and cooled things down by reaching up on tip-toe

*Strange Harmony*

to give her Uncle a quick peck on the cheek. She took the key off him firmly, and opened the door, easily slipping out of his rather half-hearted attempt to hold her up against the door-jamb.

"See you next week, Ray," Maggie called back archly, "'Bye," and she skipped lightly down the stairs and let herself out of the front door.

As she walked down the drive, she found herself feeling both excited and flattered by her Uncle's rather surprising advances. She also noticed a peculiar kind of almost over-whelming euphoria and relief that she had been able to control the situation, having been found on the bed, and drinking gin, *and* still escaping intact from what had been her first really adult sexual encounter.

She felt really good about herself, so she was bursting to tell someone about her adventure and decided that Karen Thomas might provide the most willing and interested ear.

# Chapter 8
# Karen Escapes

It was five o'clock, so Karen pulled the blind down on the door of her café and put the 'closed' notice up. It had not been a busy afternoon: a couple of the Irish navvies had called in for their usual tea of eggs on toast, and a few householders had come to buy the odd grocery from the shop attached to the café.

That was the part of her business that Karen hoped to expand, but so far she had been refused permission to extend the building. She had not given up hope, however, for she was an astute business woman and had been busy getting some more of the Councillors on her side. Her time would come.

Then, as she rearranged some of the chairs around the window table she saw Maggie skipping down the road towards the shop. She opened the door and welcomed Maggie in,

"Hullo. What's up? Bouncing down the road like that."

"My Uncle Ray's just tried to rape me." Whispered Maggie excitedly.

"MAGGIE! WHAT ARE YOU SAYING?"

*Strange Harmony*

"Oh, it's alright. He didn't get anywhere. I fought him off easily."

"MAGGIE! This is serious. Tell me what happened. Exactly!"

Maggie's recounted her recent experience with her Uncle—the words tumbling out of her mouth. Karen could see the girl was over-excited and was probably enjoying embroidering the story a bit, but she was really concerned for her.

"So he didn't actually rape you?"

"I didn't let him, don't you worry." Maggie giggled. "He only got as far as my leg."

"Maggie. Don't fool about. Ray's a big bloke. He'd get his way with you if he really wanted to."

"Oh. He really wanted to, all right. He was up for it. I could see."

"You were on his bed, you say? That was a stupid thing to do."

"I didn't know he was coming home early, did I? He just found me there."

"And you think he came home early especially to try it on with you?"

"Looking back on it, I'm sure he did. He's sort of been hinting at it for some time."

"And you under age too. AND his niece. Didn't that frighten you?"

"No. Not really. I found it quite exciting really."

"Now you come here and listen to me, my girl. This is serious. Ray Roberts can be dangerous. Let me tell you what he did to me."

Karen took the girl into her living room behind the shop and sat her down firmly in an arm chair. There, quietly and unemotionally she told her how, when she was a young girl, just a little older than Maggie, she had gone to Ray's office at his invitation to talk to him about her having a job at the mine. Ray had seduced her, right there in his office.

He subsequently had given her a secretarial job and they had carried on a secret affair for almost a year. Unfortunately, Karen had become pregnant and Ray had 'bought her off' as he had put it. He had explained to her that he could never leave his wife, Megan, and as they had so far been able to keep their affair secret and within the confines of the office, Karen would always have to hide the identity of the father.

So she had had her son as quietly as she could, and had brought him up herself for the last fourteen years, experiencing a mixture of ostracism and kindness from the people of the village. Luckily, she had benefited from her mother and father's support.

Maggie responded in amazement,

"So Uncle Ray's your Ronald's father!"

"Yes. But you must keep that a secret. Promise me Maggie. PROMISE ME!"

"Of course, Karen. But you were very lucky your father and mother were so good. My father won't be like that, I know. If I got pregnant I'd be out of the house like a shot."

"That's why I wanted to talk to you about it. You may have got away with it this time, but Ray Roberts is a very determined man, and he's used to getting his own way. You'll need to be careful."

"I will, Karen, don't worry. I can look after myself."

"I hope so, for your sake. Just don't give him the opportunity."

"Well," Maggie laughed, "He won't find me on his bed again, that's for sure."

"Good. But just watch him. That's what I mean."

Her warning was interrupted by a knock on the shop door. Karen went through the shop, and immediately ran back to Maggie in the living room.

"It's him. Ray Roberts!" she whispered.

"Speak of the devil." Maggie replied. Karen walked quickly back to the shop.

"You stay in here. I'll keep him in the shop. Just be quiet, I might need you.

Maggie looked at her quizzically but closed the door between the rooms, leaving a little gap to peep through.

"Karen. I need to talk to you about something." Ray moved his big frame through the door, brushing past her, as Karen opened it.

"Come on in, Ray," said Karen pointedly, closing the door behind him.

"Can I get you tea or something?" She could smell the gin on his breath as he passed her, so she didn't expect a positive response, but she did notice his face was even more florid than usual and he seemed somewhat agitated, she assumed he was still feeing the effects of his unsuccessful encounter with Maggie.

"No thanks Karen. I just needed to see you."

"O.K. How can I help you?"

"It's more about how I can help you." They both sat down, Karen deliberately keeping a table between them, "You know I felt bad about your shop extension, I'm sure we can get the decision reversed if you play your cards right."

"And how can I do that?"

"Well, we were good friends once, I was hoping we might . . . ."

"We were rather more than good friends as you well know, and I've got Ronald to prove it!" She retorted, venom in her voice.

"That was unfortunate, but Megan was alive then, I couldn't do anything about it."

"You didn't want to do anything about it, you mean."

"Well, that's water under the bridge. Now that Megan's gone, things could be different . . . ."

"You're actually suggesting we could start again?"

"Yes. We could both benefit—and you always said it was good between us . . . ."

"You had your chance, Ray Roberts. It may have been good for you, but I've paid the price ever since. Once bitten, as they say."

"But Karen. I want to make it up to you."

"No chance. And after what you've just done to my father you'll never be able to make it up to me. I've struggled for the last fourteen years on my own and things were at last beginning to get easier. Now he's in prison. You're the last thing I need just now Ray Roberts. I won't make the same mistake again, believe me."

"I'm sorry to hear that, Karen, because I need you, and you're still a very attractive woman. If you won't do it the easy way, you know full well I have other ways of getting what I want." Ray stood up and started to move around the table towards her. Karen, remembering what the younger Ray Roberts of her youth was capable of doing, watched him warily and moved away from him.

He moved swiftly around the table and pinned her to the wall, holding her arms spread wide above her head, his body tight up against hers. As she felt his knee trying to force her legs apart she brought her own knee upwards sharply. He gasped, let her go and bent over in pain. She struggled away from him. But he was too quick for her. He caught her right arm roughly and pulled her to the ground. He rolled on top of her, his sixteen stone knocking most of the breath from her body. She could hardly move. Although she was a strong, fit woman, she was no match for her assailant.

With almost no breath left, she turned her head to the door and gasped hoarsely,

"MAGGIE. HELP!"

Maggie, having watched the whole episode with surprise, now really alarmed, leapt into the room and shouted,

"UNCLE RAY!. What do you think you're doing?" She pulled at his shoulders as he looked up in surprise at her abrupt entrance. He let Karen go and stood up, his faced suffused and angry, staring at Maggie.

"Thanks, Maggie," said Karen, getting to her feet, "I had a feeling I might need you. Ray Roberts, you clear off now before I shout for help and let the whole village know what you are really like."

"You tell anybody about this and you'll be sorry—both of you!"

He glared at the two women and then stormed out of the shop and slammed the door behind him.

"Wow! That was a narrow escape," sighed Karen, "But now you know what he's prepared to do. It's just as well you were here—I told you you'll have to watch him."

"It's amazing. I've known him since I was a little girl and I never would have thought . . . ."

"You never do with men. That's what I was trying to tell you just before he came. You've got to look after yourself Maggie. You may have got away with it this time, but it's never good to be too confident. You may not always be able to cope with them, so just be on your guard, that's all I'm saying."

"Thanks, Karen. I'm glad I told you about what happened in Uncle Ray's bedroom. There's no one else I can really talk to—but I'll keep Ronald as our secret, don't worry."

# *Chapter 9*
# Deadly Games

The gang of a dozen or so young boys ran down from the village to the big field, 'Cae Mawr', as they still called it, even though the new railway track had sliced it in half.

Their ages ranged from about eight years to ten. Davy had reached his eighth birthday only the week before and had been proud to be allowed to join his brother, Jack, in the gang. Their parents were Hannah and William Pritchard, whose two elder boys were working down the mine, as they had done since they were twelve, along side their father

It was Saturday and the boys shouted excitedly to each other as they ran, glad to be free from the confines of school and determined to enjoy their freedom. For some of them, that freedom was quite soon to be drastically curtailed when they joined Harry and Jim, hacking coal out of the depths of the mine for twelve hours each day.

For a time however, they could enjoy themselves in the big field, where, before the track had bisected it, they had usually played football. Today, however, they were looking forward to playing their new game, racing the coal train

*Strange Harmony*

as it steamed down the track from the mine higher up the valley.

Along this length of the track it was safe for the boys to play, because the mine owners had put wooden rails on each side of the railway specifically to keep people off it. However, as the track entered the trees at the bottom of the field, the wooden rails stopped: it had been too difficult and too expensive to continue them all the way through the wood.

Nor had the owners bothered to guard the track as it emerged from the wood through a kind of gorge onto the flat fields again: they had assessed that it did not warrant the extra cost. Unfortunately, they had calculated without any understanding of the abandoned, adventurous spirit of the young boys of the village.

The boys galloped noisily after the new train, which steamed, full of coal, through the field and into the wood. In the wood, the dry, Autumn leaves crunched under the boys pounding feet, but they had to dodge around the trees and were no match for the train. They cheered it goodbye as they got to the gorge, Davy lagging behind them, for he had had some difficulty keeping up with his brother and the bigger boys, not just because he was a slower runner, but because of the new boots, which he had had for his birthday.

At least they were new for him. In fact they had already been handed down twice through his older brothers, but they were proper boots, with metal studs in them, just like his dad's, and he was very proud of them. The fact that they were really too big for him, and he had difficulty with the long laces, did not matter. He would be the last to admit to the other boys that it was his new boots that slowed him down.

They got to the field beyond the gorge and had a rest to get their breath back, lying out flat on the lush grass at the side of the track.

"Right," said brother Jack, leaning up on his elbow, "When it comes back we'll pretend it's a bull and we're all bull-fighters." (They'd heard about Spain from some of the men of the village who had been there to fight in the war, and the stories about bull-fighting had fired their imaginations.)

"Yes," answered one of the older boys, "and we'll jump across the track in front of it."

"The last one the winner!" Shouted one of the others.

"Right. But be careful when you jump," warned Jack, "Davy, you'd better stay here on this side. It's too dangerous for you."

"No fear. I want to beat the bull too. I'm coming with you."

Then suddenly they heard the engine's whistle as it came round the bend just below them. What they didn't properly appreciate was that the train, relieved of its burden of coal, was able to travel considerably more quickly on its return journey,

"Now. Get ready!" commanded Jack. The boys gathered obediently in a group on the side of the track. The train approached quickly, surrounded by its usual cloud of steam. The boys crouched ready for the jump across the track. The first, more timorous ones, went well before the train reached them. The driver saw what they were doing and shook his fist at them.

"Get away from the track, you stupid idiots!" He shouted. The main body of boys ignore him and leapt across the track just before the engine reached them. Jack was the last. At least he thought he was last. Until he heard a terrifying scream. It was Davy. He had tripped over his boot-lace and had fallen right across the track just as the train got to him.

Jack looked around even before he hit the ground,

"NO! DAVY!" his own scream was even louder than his brother's. Then the train was past them. Jack looked down in horror at his brother's mangled body, spread-eagled on the side of the track. Some of the boys started to cry at the awful sight. Davy lay still, his little body covered in blood.

"I'll get the ambulance!" Shouted the engine driver, and carried on up the track, leaving the boys in horrified silence. Jack hardly heard him, for he was already running home as fast as his legs would take him. Through the wood, up the big field and into the village street. As he reached his house in the terrace he shouted,

"MAM. MAM! It's Davy!" His mother came out to meet him.

"What on earth's happened?" She asked as she saw her son's ashen face.

"It's Davy. The train hit him and he's dead!"

"The train hit him? Don't be silly, Jack!" she tried to calm the boy, but soon realised he was serious. "Where is he? Where did it happen? Quick! TELL ME."

"Down at the end of the wood. We were just playing. He's dead. HE'S DEAD MAM!" The boy dissolved into tears, "I told him to stay on his side But he wouldn't." He sobbed as his mother hugged him. She answered, her heart fluttering madly,

"You stay here with Ruth. I'll go down to see him."

"You don't want to see him, Mam. He's all broken."

Mary's step faltered when she saw her son's anguish, but this made her run all the faster out of the village, down the big field and through the woods. There, at the end of the wood, in the field below the gorge, she saw the broken body of her youngest boy, his left leg almost amputated, just hanging onto his torso by threads, his head bent over his shoulder at a frightening, unnatural angle. The gang of boys, shocked into silence, looked on, as Mary let out an agonised wail and gathered up the little body into her arms.

*Strange Harmony*

She said nothing to the frightened boys but just walked up through the woods and back home with her precious burden. Her tortured mind was in a whirl. Every morning she would wave her husband and her two eldest sons goodbye. Every morning she would have a great fear in her heart as they went off to work in the mine, knowing they may not return to her alive. She had never once been concerned about her youngest son, who always left her for school, happy and carefree. And now he was the one she had lost.

Her body was wracked with her sobbing as she got to the village street. A crowd of women had gathered as the news had spread quickly. They looked at Davy's body in horror as Mary took the boy into the house.

By this time the men were returning from their shift down the mine. William Thomas ran into his house and stood and stared aghast at his wife holding the shattered body of their youngest. He stifled a shuddering sob, for the over-riding emotion he felt was one of deep anger. He shouted at the crowd who had come into the room with him,

"We told them putting the railway so close to the village would be dangerous. Now look what's happened. Our little Davy has paid for it"

"The railway's always been bad news. First our land. Now this." The crowd had been joined by some of the

*Alun Jones*

farmers' and one of them was quick to add fire to their rising anger. Another added,

"That settles it. We've been looking for an excuse ever since they jailed Huw. This is it. Follow me men."

With that, a group of men broke away from the crowd and started to move down towards the wood. They had planned what to do after the riot of the opening day; they had just needed a trigger. Davy's death had supplied it. Now some of them stopped off at their houses to pick up saws and ropes.

"Quiet now." Their leader commanded, "We don't want the bloody railway police up at the pit-head to hear us. It'll be dark soon. They mustn't find out 'til the morning."

The group of angry men soon got to the gorge below the wood. There they selected three of the biggest trees that overhung the track and set to with their saws. Some of them threw ropes around the trees to make certain they fell across the track where they could do most damage.

Eventually, after a lot of hot, sweaty sawing, the men watched the trees fall with a crash and suppressed a satisfied cheer. They didn't want the police to interfere this time, one of them in jail was bad enough, and this was only the start of the actions they had planned.

# *Chapter 10*
# Phoebe Takes A Risk'

Bryn and Phoebe met in the practice room of the Workmen's Hall in the centre of the village, as they usually did before choir practice to prepare the music they were going to rehearse.

This was the last practice before the competition that Bryn had been slowly working towards over his three years with the choir, so he was feeling just a little apprehensive. Phoebe looked at him anxiously, as they both sat at the old piano,

"Bryn. Do you think things are meant to happen?"

"Of course not! You know I don't believe all that sort of stuff. Things just happen. Why are you asking me that now?"

"Well I often wonder if you were *meant* to come here to be our conductor, and whether Megan was *meant* to die in that practice, and if we are really *meant* to win lots of competitions and become famous."

"You *are* a funny woman. You can believe it was all arranged by that God of yours if it makes you feel better, but the *fact* is I came here because I heard the choir in that concert—that was chance; I reckoned the choir had potential—that was professional judgement; I heard that you were looking for a new conductor and I was offered the position—that was opportunity. That's all there was to it!"

"I suppose so. But do you really think we can win?"

"I am sure we can. I wouldn't be working at it if I didn't think so. It's just a matter of weaning you all off all those simple, sentimental pieces you used to sing and getting you to tackle some real music."

"But, Bryn . . . ."

"*And* building in some discipline and getting you to strive for technical excellence, of course. That's what choirs should really be about—striving for excellence, and that's why competitions are good for us. And *that's* why I'm here—to win competitions with *this choir*!"

"But Bryn, not everyone wants the choir to do new things and improve, as you say, nor to compete with other choirs. Ray and Megan Roberts to start with, they've never wanted to do that, and they've always felt it's their choir. Neither of them has been happy about all your changes, you know that very well—but just listen to me, I'm still talking as though Megan is alive"

"That's been the problem; no vision," replied Bryn, ignoring her reference to Megan, "They're just happy for the choir to repeat the same old things year after year. But *I'm* in charge of the choir now, and I've got a vision of it becoming really famous, *and* I intend to achieve that vision somehow or other."

"But you won't achieve it if Ray Roberts can help it, especially now he thinks you were to blame for his wife's death."

"That's ridiculous. I did nothing to contribute to her death. Though, I must admit, it'll be much easier without her. And it would be even easier without *him* too, but surely you realise I wouldn't have got rid of her deliberately. There are simpler means of getting my own way. I can deal with Ray Roberts, don't you worry."

Their conversation was interrupted by the first members of the choir arriving and taking their usual seats. Soon others followed, and Bryn arranged his music ready for the practice.

They normally started promptly at seven: Bryn insisted on promptness as a part of the choir's discipline, but this evening, by five past seven, he looked around the room disapprovingly and asked,

"Where are all the tenors and basses, then?" At least half of the men's chairs were empty. There was an embarrassed silence. Then Dr. Morgan volunteered,

"I think you'll find that Ray Roberts told them not to come if they valued their jobs in the mine." Bryn blanched,

"You mean he's threatened them with the sack if they come to practice?"

"Yes!" came back the chorus from the other men.

"You can't blame them for not coming," said Dr. Morgan. "It's his response to you not going to Megan's funeral, I imagine. He said he'd pay you back—this is his way of doing it."

"But he wouldn't do that to the choir, surely. He knows we've got the competition next week!" Answered Bryn, exasperated and angry now, but doing his best to hide his fury.

"He 's not doing it to the choir. HE'S DOING IT TO YOU!" replied Dr. Morgan, "He's obviously out to break you—he's said so."

"Well he won't succeed. We'll go ahead with the competition. The ladies will just have to hold the volume back a bit to balance the parts. We'll beat him yet, if he wants to play that game. Now, let's start with Parry's 'I was glad'—that's the piece we need to polish most."

The depleted choir opened their copies, Phoebe played the introduction and they burst into the first jubilant chords of the competition's most demanding item.

At the end of the second page, Bryn held up his hand to stop the singing,

"Good. Good." He said, "But the sopranos are too loud. I know I said let these first lines rip, but we must listen to each other. Our overall volume will now have to depend on what the basses can produce, and gentlemen, for goodness sake don't force it because there's so few of you—there's no need to shout—a smooth tone is still essential. Tenors, you're doing well, keep it up."

The practice proceeded smoothly, Bryn encouraged the singers and carefully corrected the few remaining technical aspects of the piece, for they had worked hard on it, and on the other competition items for some weeks, and by this time, they knew them well. He concluded the practice after about an hour and a half's work,

"Well done all of you. Sing like that and we'll be O.K., but look as though you are enjoying yourselves—you all look dead worried. It'll be all right. Remember we have to communicate our skill to the judges as well as to the audience this time, so don't be afraid to look them in the eye. See you all next week. Thanks again, Phoebe."

The choir members left in twos and threes, and Bryn and Phoebe cleared up the room and began to review the practice together, as they usually did. Phoebe started a little timorously,

"Do you really think we'll be all right? There's quite a lot of men missing."

"The balance was quite good actually, considering. As long as the sopranos keep it back a bit we'll be all right, but there's some stiff competition. We'll need to put all we've got into it."

"You know you told us about communicating our skill, do you think that's enough, Bryn, especially for the competition?" Phoebe tried to draw Bryn out.

"Of course its not only a matter of skill. For competitions, choirs have got to demonstrate technical excellence as well as skill, *and* reveal their musical understanding of the pieces, at the same time. But it's mainly my job to draw that out of them when we compete."

She looked at the strong lines of his face, and, sensitive to the way he was trying to cope with the current set-back, she risked taking their discussion deeper,

"My old teacher always said that performing music was about skill *and* soul. Music that is all skill and no soul is dead, she used to say".

"Oh, don't give me that nonsense. I gave all that soul business up when I left Sunday School. Put all your mind and heart into the music—yes. But soul—that's beyond me. As far as I'm concerned there's no such thing—I'll only believe I've got one when you can prove it to me."

"Or when you *feel* it." Added Phoebe gently. "We've all got souls whether we realise it or not." She went on quietly, "Some are a bit shrivelled up a bit, that's all. They just need some new stimulation." She blanched a little at her unusual forthrightness, for she knew all about his strong views on anything that smacked of what he felt was 'religious'.

However, she felt confident enough to broach the subject at this crucial stage in the choir's development, because she had grown very fond of Bryn, and actually felt that he was quite limited in his approach both to music and to life, in spite of his obvious musical talent and expertise. She had never had the temerity to tell him so directly before, but because of the present crisis he was experiencing with Ray Roberts, she thought it might be a good time to try to help him again see how he had been limiting himself.

He had told her a bit about his childhood in one of their meetings, so she could understand how he felt as he did. His father had been killed in a tragic accident when working in the mine. Bryn was ten at the time. His mother had died two years later, some said of a broken heart, and he had been brought up by a rather forbiddingly strict grandmother, who was a fervent chapel-goer. All her persuasion and pressure to get him to chapel had failed. As he often said to his communist party comrades years later, when he needed help most, religion had given him nothing. Phoebe could readily appreciate why he had abandoned his grandmother's chapel, and her religion when he was a child of twelve—he felt that he had been abandoned by the very God she and her chapel were trying to portray.

"You know you'll never convert me." He said, with a laugh.

"I'm not interested in your conversion," she answered, "But I *am* interested in the music we're trying to make together. I want it to be the best we can possibly make it. It's got to be, if we're going to be successful, competing with all those other choirs.

"It'll be the best all right, and we'll be successful. But I'll lead it and you accompany it. Then we know where we stand." She knew he did not mean to be unkind, so she dropped the subject as they strolled out of the hall together.

# Chapter 11
# The Singing Lesson

Bryn welcomed Maggie warmly into the tiny music room in his flat above the newsagent and book shop in High Street, the main street of the village. The room had music scattered everywhere and the floor space was almost totally taken over by the baby grand piano, which was his pride and joy.

It was a Richard Lipp and he had bought it in an auction in Cardiff, the first he had ever been to; he still remembered the excitement of making the final winning bid. He'd wanted that piano badly: it had to be a baby grand to help confirm his status as one of the leading music teachers in the area and it never failed to impress prospective students. Maggie stared at it in amazement, and smiled at Bryn,

"This is so kind of you Mr. Griffiths, taking me on for singing lessons."

"Please call me Bryn, Maggie, there's no formality here, and as I told you, you have a beautiful voice. You could go far with it if you wanted to."

"Oh, thank you, Mr. Griffiths, but doing them for nothing, I meant. I was sorry that Dad said he wasn't going to pay for me just to learn to sing."

"Think nothing of it. It's my job to spot potential for the choir and to bring it on. I'm glad to be able to do it. I've done it for lots of members of my choirs in the past, so don't worry. I think you can develop into a very good soloist in time. That would be my ambition for you, then I would benefit too"

"That would be wonderful. I promise I'll practice hard."

"Good. Well first of all you've got to learn to breathe properly. You can practice that all the time. It's basic for good singing. Now let's start."

Bryn started the young girl on some exercises to develop her breathing. He put his hand on her diaphragm to show her how to use it properly in producing the best sound. It surprised her that they had started the lesson just by learning to breathe differently, so she was glad when they got on to actual singing. Even then her new teacher only allowed her to demonstrate how she pitched and produced one note at a time, by playing a note on the piano and asking her to sing it out and hold it for as long as she could. Bryn explained to her,

"You see, Maggie, it's essential not only to pitch each note absolutely perfectly, but to hold the pitch for as long the music demands. I'll let you borrow this tuning fork, then you can practise pitching the note and holding it for a complete breath, then strike the fork again to check that you are still in tune. There's nothing worse than a singer who can't keep in tune.

It was only for a very short time at the end of the lesson that Bryn allowed her to sing a simple song, and Maggie obviously showed that she had not expected all the exercises,

"It's all right, Maggie, we won't be just practising techniques all the time, voices are for singing songs after all, not just for making musical noises. You won't be bored, I promise you."

"I'm sure I shan't, and I'm so grateful. I've always wanted to sing. I've really enjoyed it."

They were both sitting by the piano by this time and the girl was looking across at her teacher with open and unembarrassed admiration shining in her bright, blue eyes. Bryn was very aware of her proximity; she was a very attractive, blonde girl, and he had heard from some of the men in the choir that she loved to flirt with them, often quite provocatively. So he moved away from her imperceptibly for he was also aware of the peculiar chemistry and attraction that could flow between young pupils and their teachers. Although he was well experienced in keeping such relationships on a strictly professional level, he also knew the risks involved. He would have to be careful with this one too.

As he looked at the young freshness sitting next to him, his mind went back to a similar situation in his last school. It was only a momentary memory, but, because it still hurt him acutely, he could see the young girl clearly. She had looked very like Maggie and had smiled at him in the same attractive way. Little did he realise after she joined his class, that, in her habit of staying behind in the classroom after each lesson she had an ulterior motive that would lead to such anguish for him.

He had insisted on keeping their relationship strictly on a teacher—pupil basis, but the girl wanted more. Much more. And when he had remonstrated with her she had gone to the Headmaster and complained that Bryn had molested her. There had followed an awful time of investigation involving the Governors and the police, throughout which he had protested his innocence.

Eventually it had transpired that the girl had a reputation with the boys of the school for being 'easy' and the other teachers had confirmed that she often behaved in an inappropriately provocative way; but the final evidence that had cleared Bryn of any guilt had been revealed by one of her friends, who she had crossed, and who, as a result, had admitted that she had heard the girl boasting that 'she would fix Mr. Griffiths' for not responding to her advances.

Although Bryn had come out of the awful experience, as the Governors had said, 'without a stain on his

*Strange Harmony*

character', it had affected him deeply and he had resigned from the school. But that was four years ago, in another valley many miles away, and in another life, as far as he was concerned.

Here, in his new village community he would put his energies into becoming famous through developing the best choir in Wales. If he also landed the organist job at the Cathedral which he had just auditioned for, that would be icing on the cake.

As he saw Maggie to the door, attractive as she was, he resolved to make certain there would be nothing she, or anyone else, could complain about in their relationship. The look that Maggie gave him as she left promised no such resolution on her part.

# Chapter 12
# Failure

"I am utterly and totally humiliated!" Bryn exploded as he walked away from the competition hall with Phoebe and the rest of the choir

"Oh, Bryn, don't take it like that." Said Phoebe, trying to console him.

"But I DO take it like that. In our first competition, to end up fourth out of five choirs—it could hardly be worse, could it?"

"The adjudicator said a lot of nice things about us, though, didn't he. Remember? He said our overall intonation was good and our phrasing was beautiful and . . . ."

"But he spotted that the balance between the parts was suspect straight away, and he thought that the bass line in 'I was glad' was not firm enough. NOT FIRM ENOUGH, INDEED!"

"But that wasn't the basses' fault. With only nine out of our usual seventeen singing with us you would expect it to be different. They did their best"

"Our best just wasn't good enough, that's what riles me, and it wasn't our fault at all. It's Ray Robert's fault entirely! Even the tenors are thinner than we need them to be. I'll get even with him, don't you worry."

"You know, I'm surprised at Uncle Ray. I didn't think he could be so vindictive; just because you missed Megan's funeral."

"Oh, he's after me for more than that. He knows I'm taking his choir off him and I'm going to make something of it at last, after his thirty years' stranglehold. He's vindictive all right. He's got a nasty, cruel streak in him. But we've just got to recruit more men somehow or other—or get Robert's workers back to practices. We can't go on as we are."

Phoebe looked at him anxiously, and agreed with him,

"You're right, we can't, especially as we've got the Swansea Eisteddfod to compete in, next month. We must get some more men by then."

"You're right Phoebe, I'd almost forgotten about Swansea because of today's disaster."

"Bryn! It wasn't a disaster. It was a good first try in difficult circumstances."

"It was a disaster. Let's face it—we lost. And the worst part wasn't just the adjudication, it was the smirk on Emyr Jenkins' face when his choir took first prize and he looked at me as though I was a beginner. He's never beaten me before with my other choirs. That's another reason I'll never forgive Ray Roberts—putting me through all that humiliation, and in front of the other conductors."

"The problem is, he'll never forgive you either: you'll never get his men to come back to practices except over his dead body"

"Now that might not be such a bad idea!" Bryn answered thoughtfully.

"Oh, Bryn. I wish you didn't feel like that about Ray. Apart from the problem of not having enough men in the choir, you and Ray, bearing each other grudges like you do, can't do much good to the quality of our singing."

"What on earth do you mean?"

"Well I think that if there is any disharmony between the people of the choir there'll be a kind of disharmony in the music we make."

"That's ridiculous."

"It's not ridiculous. You agree that it is important that you and I get on well because we're at the heart of the music. We've got to be in harmony, haven't we? We either help the music hang together, or we let it fall apart. You know how it sounds when that happens—and how it feels.

"I can agree with that, but we're *leading* the music. The members of the choir are just producing the sound."

"Oh, Bryn! They're not *just producing the sound.* That's the whole point—WE'RE ALL DOING IT TOGETHER! Or we're supposed to be—we're trying to re-create the music the composer originally created. Granted, he heard it in his heart or mind or something, but the music came from his soul."

"You're right about his whole heart and mind needing to be in his music. I know that because I've done some composing myself, but . . . ."

"Well there you are then." Phoebe continued, quite excited now, "It must have come from *your* soul, as well!"

"That's just nonsense. I haven't got one."

"Oh yes you have. Everyone has! I believe that music comes from the soul of the universe: it's a song in the heart of God, and when a composer hears its strange harmony he can reproduce it in his own music, at least sometimes."

"But . . . ." Bryn tried to interject again, but the little accompanist rushed on,

"Then, if a choir can only catch an echo of that same, strange harmony as they sing, their listeners will be transported too, and it all comes together in a really wonderful musical experience for them all. But a choir can only do that if they get along really well with each other. If there's any bad feeling in the choir it'll ruin the music. At least that's what I think."

"You may be right." Bryn 's voice was full of doubt, so Phoebe looked straight at him, she was gaining confidence now, and continued,

"I *am* right. And that's why, however big or small the choir is, if you and Ray Roberts, or anyone else for that matter, are quarrelling all the time we'll never make really good music—and we probably won't win any competitions."

"Hah! It's much more than a quarrel, as you call it. It feels more like war, so either he or I will have to go, because we ARE going to win competitions"

"Well, *you're* not going to go, are you. So it'll have to be Ray. But he'll certainly not leave on his own, not after having had his own way with the choir for thirty years."

"Then I'll have to get rid of him, won't I? If what you say about him spoiling the quality of our singing is right, then he's just got to go. And the quicker the better."

Bryn looked at his accompanist in a new light,

"Thanks Phoebe, you've helped me make my mind up."

# Chapter 13
# The Explosion

Early the next morning an enormous explosion shook the whole village. Hannah Pritchard sat up abruptly in her bed. The first explosion was followed by two others that rattled the ornaments on her bedside table,

"OH NO! . . . . WILLIAM!" She shouted in alarm, unable to stop herself. Her whole body trembled and her heart pounded.

She knew exactly what had happened. It was the pit explosion she had feared for the last five years. William and her two elder boys were working at that very moment in the new coal-seam over a thousand feet below the surface. They were probably lying trapped under tons of fallen rock and coal right underneath where she now lay shivering with fear in their bed, where William had left her only two hours before to get ready for his early morning shift.

Five years ago her father and two brothers had died in just such an explosion. They had been caught in the blast of air and the rush of flame resulting from a tiny spark in the gas-laden air of the dark under-ground labyrinth that was their daily place of work. The three of them had suffered horrible burns and had never recovered after being brought to the surface by their rescuers. Twenty eight other husbands, sons and brothers of the village had died in the explosion at the same time, asphyxiated by the clouds of dust swirling through the coal seams and levels, or burnt and buried alive as the safety timbers around them caught fire and the roofs of the narrow seams out of which they had been digging the coal, fell in. She could still see all of them lying side by side at the pit-head.

She felt the horror of what was happening to her William, and to Harry and Jim, their sons, yet only twelve and eleven years old, right now caught dead or alive in the holocaust of this new explosion. She knew exactly what they would be experiencing. William had luckily escaped the last explosion five years ago, with just a broken arm and superficial burns, but the three days entombed hundreds of feet under-ground with his friends dying all around him one after the other from all kinds of horrible injuries and burns, had left deep marks on him which not even the relief of being brought to the surface alive had been able to eradicate.

Far from it. Even after describing to her what he had gone though in graphic detail many, many times, he still sometimes woke up at her side at night, sweating and shouting as he re-lived the terrible experience. And now it was happening again. He had gone back down the pit, of course. He had no other means of supporting their growing family. But every day since that awful time she had waved him off to work with a deep, deep fear in her heart that there would be another explosion down the pit and that this time her William would not return to her alive.

Shivering and sweating at the same time with growing anxiety and over-active imagining, she threw on some clothes, ran frantically out of their little house and joined the crowd of other wives and mothers who were running towards the pit-head, all too afraid of what they would find.

As fast as the women ran towards the mine, there was one figure who out-stripped them all. Ray Roberts had been woken by the explosion too, sleeping comfortably in his grand house in the upper village. He too was horrified at the thought of another explosion at the mine. He too was remembering the last one with growing alarm as he ran.

Like all the women he too could easily imagine what was happening. But his apprehension was of a quite different kind from that etched starkly into the faces of the women behind him. He was not worried to death about what any near relatives or friends were going through. He was worried for himself.

Five years ago he had been the newly appointed manager of the mine, and promoted to the Board of owners. Five years ago he personally had been found guilty of negligence and responsible with the other Board members for the disaster. The grinding official enquiry had probed his every action or more tellingly, his in-action, and he had never forgotten the feelings of humiliation that the public criticism had aroused.

So he ran towards the mine with a heart full of a different set of emotions from those of the terrified women. The £25 fine for his negligent safety management had never worried him. The owners on the Board had paid that anyway, as they had happily paid their own trivial fine of £10 for their corporate share in responsibility for the unfortunate accident.

He had also coped easily with the veiled condemnation of his workers and their families in the village; he found their obvious disgust at his re-instatement as mine manager by his Board after the enquiry, a little more difficult to handle. They all knew it was a reward for the way he had personally borne the brunt of the questions and the criticism of the Inspectors of Mines in charge of the official enquiry. He and the Board had got off very lightly.

However, he had never forgotten the deep anxiety and the unexpected nervousness the grilling by the mining experts during the enquiry, had left him with. This time it would be far worse, for they would have the recent Mines Act to back their questioning. It had been passed eventually in 1911, just two years ago, after many long debates in the House of Commons by protagonists of the conflicting interests of the Mine Owners and the Trade Unions on behalf of the miners.

The rapidly increasing number of mine explosions and accidents in the expanding and immensely profitable coal-mining industry had eventually won the day for a much more regulated approach to the management of mine safety and a strict adherence to specified safety policies and practices.

As he ran, full of trepidation, Roberts knew full-well that anyone found responsible for breaking the rules and strictures of the new Act would be given a prison sentence. He also knew what a low priority he and the mine-owners had given to the new regulations, as Morgan, his safety engineer was forever pointing out to him. Some of the recommendations of the enquiry of five years ago had not yet been fully implemented, let alone all the new regulations that were now required.

He, and the owners to whom he owed his livelihood and status, had been much more interested in developing the new seams of the mine and earning even greater profits from the increased production of coal than in following all the requirements of the Act and in providing a safe working environment for their men. As the official enquiry had pointedly declared: 'men come cheap'. And that still clearly applied, Act or no Act. But the possibility of a prison sentence if he were found responsible for the explosion this time, sharpened his apprehension considerably. As he ran he was totally and starkly anxious about his own future. His shirt hung wet on his back and his breathing was laboured. The hundred and twenty men who were underground facing all kinds of physical and psychological horrors did not form part of his otherwise unbounded trepidation.

# Chapter 14
## The Pit-Head

Roberts and the growing crowd of terrified, anxious women had been joined on the way from the village by a number of men who had been on the previous night shift and had been going to bed when they heard the explosion. They had thrown on their working clothes from the night before and were now keenly intent on getting to the scene of the disaster as fast as they could to be of whatever help they could to their stricken comrades, trapped a thousand feet below them.

They all could see the immediate results of the explosion long before they reached the gates of the mine. The great wheels at the head of the main shaft, whose inexorable turning signalled the villagers' continued daily employment and pay-check, were ominously still. The huge cage, which took the miners and their equipment down to their dark, dusty, daily toil, and brought back to the surface the coal which increasingly poured the considerable profits of the enterprise into the pockets of the owners, sat bent and twisted at the top of the shaft where it had been brought to a shuddering halt after being driven, accelerating all the way up the shaft, by the gigantic blast of the explosion.

Over the pit-head lay a great pall of smoke and dust which added an ominous back-drop to the frightening scene that now presented itself to the approaching runners. Apprehension etched into their faces, the women immediately ran through the gates to the side of the cage where already six bodies had been laid out by the gathering crowd of shocked fellow-workers. An awful wailing rose from the unfortunate wives and mothers who discovered their loved ones amongst these early victims, their friends sympathetically embracing them, only too aware that their own time of tragedy might soon follow. The wailing added to the noise of the increasing number of men rushing around, totally disorganised, not knowing what to do next to help their other comrades trapped in the workings of the mine, far below the surface, but all very willing to shout loud, strident orders to their colleagues milling around the pit-head.

This was the terrifying, fear-filled chaos that confronted Roberts as he led the women through the gates of the mine and ran to the head of the shaft. For a brief second he stood appalled at the scene of shouting, running men. Then he drew himself up to his full impressive height and bellowed above the din,

"All you men, stop where you are!" The men immediately stood stock still at his command. "Now get into groups of six. You two groups," pointing at the first groups to form up, "Get over to Mr. Jenkins there, and help him straighten out the cage—we've got to get it working if we're to get the survivors up to the surface. Now MOVE!" He shouted encouragement at the men and gave orders to the senior engineer, Jacob Jenkins, who was valiantly trying to straighten the bars of the cage with crowbars on his own.

"Jenkins. The rescue teams will be here soon. Organise some of these groups so that they're ready to help mend the cage and clear the shaft."

With that he ran across the yard through the crowd of frightened, wailing women to the changing hut and lamp-room where, he knew, the surface workers on the shift would have set up a first-aid area for the injured miners who had been blown to the surface in the cage.

There were about thirty men, lying on the floor or sitting at the tables, most of them with a variety of injuries, broken arms and legs and bloodied, cut heads because they had lost their helmets as the cage had shot to the surface like a missile and had come to an abrupt stop when it hit the steel gantry at the top of the shaft.

There was blood everywhere, and the heart rending groans from some of the more badly injured men added to the awfulness of the room, but Robert's look of horror turned to one of amazement as he saw Dr. Handel Morgan and Nurse Phoebe in the middle of the carnage, giving directions to a few first-aiders who were bending over men, temporarily straightening broken arms and legs and bandaging them up with rough splints.

"What on earth are you two doing here?" he asked peremptorily.

"What do you think we're doing?" answered the doctor, acidly.

"But how did you . . . . ?"

"We were called out on a minor injury just before seven, so we were on the spot when the explosion happened. Unlike you, lying in your bed. See what you've done again. Six dead already, and some of these ones here won't last long by the look of them. Better than last time, Mr. Roberts!" The doctor added sarcastically, staring at the mine manager with anger and antagonism.

"You mind your bloody mouth, Morgan, or you'll be needing medical attention yourself!" The doctor's unveiled accusation painfully sharpened Robert's growing feelings of impending doom, not just at the human results of the explosion around him and those still trapped underground, but at the probable findings of the inevitable enquiry that now loomed ahead of him.

"You know very well that your negligence over safety rules is the root of all the accidents in this place, and there's not even any disinfectant in this First-Aid kit. TYPICAL!"

*Strange Harmony*

Robert's face turned purple as he shouted furiously at the doctor,

"You withdraw that remark, Morgan, or I'll . . . ."

"You'll do nothing, Roberts. As usual. It's all the things you *haven't* done that have caused this explosion again. My brother Haydn has got a long list of safety things you haven't seen to. He's shown it to me, and he's down there now. And that's your fault too. If he doesn't get up alive, I'll see that the enquiry get the whole list. You're for the high jump this time. I'll see to that!"

With new fear tearing at his heart and a deep, growing, red mist clouding his mind, Roberts lost control and lifted the diminutive doctor by his coat lapels until their furious faces were level.

"I'll bloody-well kill you first, you . . . ."

"PUT HIM DOWN, Mr. Roberts," It was Phoebe defending her doctor friend and colleague by pulling at Robert's arm, who luckily regained some semblance of control, as she added quickly,

"You don't want to face charges of grievous bodily harm as well, now do you? There's enough men dead and injured round here already!"

This brought Roberts back to the awful reality surrounding him. He realised that he not only had to cope with his own fear and anxiety but he had also to establish some degree of control over the desperate

*Alun Jones*

situation the mine was in. So he dropped the little doctor uncremoniously to the ground and shouted,

"You've wasted enough of my time. Get on with your bandages. I've got to check the north face ventilation shaft. It's our only chance until the lifting gear in the main shaft is back on line."

With that he stormed out of the makeshift hospital and shouted to a group of men nearby,

"Edwards, and you men there. Come with me quick, We must see if the north shaft is clear and try to get the injured men out that way. As he turned to run, he shouted back to the men working on the gantry and cage of the main shaft,

"Any chance with the main shaft, Jenkins?"

"Yes, Boss. Nearly there. With a bit of luck she'll be on line in half-an-hour. Leave this end with me."

Roberts allowed himself a small sigh of relief as he heard the good news from Jenkins and at the same time saw members of the teams from the Rescue Centre unloading their equipment from the trucks that had arrived through the gates. At least things would be organised now, he thought.

He ran with Edwards, one of his deputies and the other men in his group the half mile or so over the dew-soaked fields to the north shaft. This shaft had been sunk partly for helping to ventilate the maze of levels and seams of the mine workings, but it had a small cage intended exactly for this purpose of emergency access. The problem was that it too may have been damaged by the terrible blast of the exploding gases deep under-ground.

So it was with great relief that Roberts and the group of apprehensive men running with him, saw the cage at the top of the shaft, a crowd of men milling around its open doorway, with one or two lying on the ground nearby.

"Evans. How many casualties? Anyone dead?" Roberts breathlessly demanded of his over-man in charge of the north seams, who was standing among the men seeing to the injured,

"None dead. Boss. Couple of minor injuries from the flames that's all. We've got everyone out from the three nearest seams. Nobody out yet from No. 4 and 5 though. It'll be a lot worse there, I guess. That's where it started I think—where we still use the old switches. I thought I heard a big roof-fall there, just as we were coming up".

Robert's usual steady heart missed a beat. The switches his over-man had referred to were the ones Haydn Morgan, his safety engineer had told him he had not ordered replacements for yet. If that became known he wouldn't have a leg to stand on. He hoped the old switches had all been buried in the fall, then nobody need know . . . . He needed to find out to put his mind at rest.

"There's about twenty-five men in 4 and 5, Boss. We were just going back to try to get at them. Want to come with us?" Asked Evans the Over-man.

"Yes, Evans. Let's go and find out how bad the fall is. Got the equipment to dig it out?"

"Right here with us, Boss. Let's go men. Twelve of us will do." Evans counted ten volunteers to go with him and the manager into the small cage. The door closed, the machinery whirred and the cage, together with its precious cargo, made its steady way down fifteen hundred feet through the solid earth to the working levels of the North seams of the mines.

# Chapter 15
# The North Shaft

Bill Pritchard leapt frantically back into the tunnel of No. 4 seam, pulling his young son Jim, with him. The roof-fall at the entrance of the seam missed them by inches. Bill turned and looked with growing dismay at the tons of rock and coal which now sealed them off from escape back to the levels of the North seams and up the ventilation shaft into the fresh air.

Jim, only ten years old and a mere four foot tall, whimpered,

"Dad. Are we buried now?"

"Don't you worry, lad. It's just a bit of a roof-fall that's all. We'll dig ourselves out in no time. The rescue team will start digging from the other end soon. You'll be home with your mum by dinner-time"

"How about Harry, Dad? Will he be buried too?"

Bill's heart lurched with fear, but he tried his best to put a confident front on. He knew that the boy's brother was more than probably dead by this time, burned by the wall of flame sweeping through No.5 seam, or else buried as the intense fire destroyed the

*Alun Jones*

pit-props and roof-timbers and brought the roof down on him.

"He'll be — all right, Jim." Bill tried to hide the anxious break in his voice,

That is what had happened to the props at the entrance to their own No.4 seam: they had caught fire and collapsed as the great flash of flame roared past them, out of No.5 seam, where it had been first ignited. It had rushed straight down the wider level that both seams opened into, and onwards, in its fatal race through the rest of the mine-workings.

The coal-face of No.4 seam where Bill and Jim and four other miners had been digging, had escaped the main fury of the blast and the flames because, although their entrance was right next to No.5 seam, their own seam went off upwards at an angle, and the rushing flames, for some reason, had passed them by. With any luck, Bill thought, the fall at the entrance to their seam, was only a small one.

From where he and Jim lay near the entrance he could just see the glimmer of light from the lamps, still alight up at the coal-face way up the seam.

"Are you all right, lads?" He called hoarsely to his comrades.

"We're O.K. Bill. How about you and Jim? We heard the fall right after the explosion. In No.5 by the sound of it. Are we trapped in here?" came the answering call.

*Strange Harmony*

"There's a bit of a fall here at the entrance. We should be able to clear it. Bring your tools down and we'll get started."

Next to him Jim started to cry, not at all convinced by his father's forced confidence,

"Dad?" He asked falteringly, "We're not going to get out are we?"

"Of coarse we are, boy. I told you, we miners are made of steel. Anyway, men don't cry, so dry your eyes and come and dig over by here."

Jim snuffled and drew his shirt sleeve across his face, only to leave a new smear of damp coal dust on his cheek. But he took heart from his father's remarks and set to, digging at the corner of the fall, to be joined almost immediately by the four other miners who had come down from the coal-face.

There was not enough room for the six of them in the narrow tunnel so they took turns, men and boys together, knowing that now their lives depended on their toiling, as did their livelihoods on normal days.

"Dad, I'm getting short of breath," said Jim quietly, obviously scared.

Bill had noticed, as had his fellow miners, that the air in the confined space of the enclosed tunnel was getting stale. The swirling dust that their shovels and picks were kicking up didn't help their breathing—dust they were used to anyway, but it was usually dampened down by water piped alongside the roof-timbers, now collapsed under the fall along with the water-pipes and electric cables.

"Here, have a sip of this cold tea." Bill poured some tea out of his flask for the boy, then soaked his coal-stained handkerchief with the remaining tea." He tried to encourage the boy . . .

"Then hold this damp cloth over your nose and mouth. It'll help your breathing."

"Thanks Dad. That's better . . . . Are we nearly through yet?"

"Almost, I should think."

"DAD! LISTEN!" The boy stood up, excited, hands to his ears.

"Stop lads!" Shouted Bill. "Listen! They're digging the other side. We're O.K. now."

The small gang of men and boys gave a weak cheer and renewed their digging, but stopped again as they heard a voice from the other side of the fall,

"Bill Pritchard. ARE YOU THERE?"

"YES!" Bill shouted, "You're almost through to us."

It seemed only a matter of minutes before the last pieces of rock between them and freedom were pulled away by the rescuers and they were able to push Jim through the hole. Moments later and the hole was big enough for the men to crawl through to collapse in relief into the arms of their comrades.

"That was close, Mr Roberts," said Bill when he saw the mine manager heading the rescue team, "The blast must have gone straight past us."

"Yes, you were lucky, Bill" replied Roberts, "We've been clearing debris and putting out fires and replacing props and timbers all the way up the level, otherwise we'd have been with you sooner. It looks as though the worst of the blast and the fire carried straight on down the levels to the main shaft. It's real chaos there. But what's happened to your face? It looks burnt to me. Your hands too. Come on, let's get back up to the surface and get you treated."

Bill looked at his hands and reached up to feel his face. Under the thick film of black dust he could see and feel his skin, all raw and tender. In the excitement and fear of his temporary burial he had not noticed the burns nor felt the pain. Now he realised that when the fire had rushed past them and they had leapt back for safety into the seam, he must have instinctively thrown his body over Jim in an attempt to save his son. He vaguely remembered looking up at the flames and putting his hands in front of his face, but had not felt the burns until now. He realised he must get them seen to soon, but he turned to the manager and said,

"Sorry Mr. Roberts, I'm not going to the surface before we've found Harry. I can't leave him down here. Hannah would never forgive me."

"He was working No.5 seam, wasn't he?"

*Alun Jones*

"Yes. He's behind that fall there." Replied Bill, pointing at the solid pile of rock that had fallen in the entrance to the seam.

"I'm afraid Bill, there's not much chance for him if he's behind that. It seems the gas that started the explosion was ignited in No.5. Nobody could have stayed alive in there. Come with us now, there's a good man. You others too. You've been through enough."

"I'll come up for treatment—I must admit these burns are beginning to throb a bit—but only if I can come straight back down. I've got to find Harry—I just know he's alive."

He turned with the others and rescuers and rescued got into the cage together and were winched to the surface.

# Chapter 16
# The Rescue Party

Bryn Griffiths woke abruptly as the explosions ripped violently through the mine workings. The dull thumps of the three eruptions shook his bed and rattled the whole of his flat above the newsagents in High Street. Like all other new-comers to the village, he had been told about the last mine disaster, which had happened five years ago, killing forty-five men, many of them choir members. So when he heard and felt the bangs he realised immediately what had happened.

His mind leapt to the already depleted tenors and basses of his present choir, and he wondered anxiously what another explosion in the mine might do to their numbers. The men's faces flashed through his imagination. In particular his anxiety rose when he remembered that Bill Pritchard, a tenor with a beautiful clear voice and one of the few really close friends he had made since coming to the village, was on the morning shift.

He got out of bed, dressed and walked briskly to the pit head, where he knew everyone in the village would be offering whatever help they could. He looked with astonishment at the dust and smoke that lay in a dark cloud over the mine, never having experienced a mine disaster before. But he could imagine what it would be like at the coal-face after the explosion, because he had spent a couple of years as a miner before getting the award to study music at the university. The thought of what the miners were going through filled him with fear and foreboding.

He picked his way through the anxious, waiting women across the yard towards the pit-head, where he could see the gangs of men working on the twisted cage. By this time all the helpers had been effectively organised so he went up to the nearest overman and asked anxiously,

"Do you know where Bill Pritchard was working this morning?"

"Not this end. Up in the north seams I think." Was the hurried reply.

"We're O.K. for help here, Bryn. They could do with you in the north shaft though, I'd guess. You'll probably find Bill there, if they've got him up yet, that is."

Bryn thanked the overman, ran past the lamp-room, and out of the yard, over the fields towards the north shaft, fearful of what he might find there, especially with how Bill Pritchard, his friend had fared in the explosion.

When he got to the head of the north shaft, he saw the cage just arriving, and a small group of men getting out of it. They were led by Roberts, the mine manager, who, as soon as he saw Bryn approaching, demanded with open antagonism,

"What are *you* doing here?"

"I'm here to help, Ray." Answered Bryn, ignoring the tone of the other man's voice and grabbing Bill Pritchard's arm,

"Bill, thank goodness you're all right. BUT LOOK AT YOUR FACE! Quick, let's get some ointment on it. He helped Bill over to the First Aid box which was on the wall of the shaft housing,

"No thanks, we mustn't use water on it . . ." he remonstrated with a surface worker who had offered a wet rag to clean the dust off Bill's face. "It's best to get ointment to cover it for now. That'll have to do until we can get him to hospital."

"No hospital for me, thanks." Responded Bill immediately, looking straight at Bryn, "Our Harry's still down there. I've got to go and get him up. That ointment will do me for now."

"You can't go back down there, Bill." The mine-manager interjected. "That roof-fall in No.5 looked far too dangerous to me. More rock could fall any moment. As it is, you could have to dig through six foot of rock to get to Harry and the rest of the gang, and anyway. they won't be alive now if the flash started in their seam." Roberts moved as if to stop Harry getting back in the cage.

*Alun Jones*

"Get out of my way, please, Mr Roberts," ordered Bill resolutely, "I know Harry is alive. I can feel it. And I'll dig through *sixty* feet of rock if need be to get my son out. Now then, who'll come with me?"

"I'm with you, Bill," said Bryn, as a dozen other hands went up.

"Thanks, butties," Bill was obviously moved by the immediate response, "But six'll do with Bryn and me for now. The rest of you can come and relieve us if we need you."

Roberts could see that there was no stopping Bill and his friends from going back down the shaft so he added,

"Best of luck to you, then. I'll go and see if we can get the ventilation fans, back on line. That should help a bit." With that, he started to return to the main shaft, while the eight would-be rescuers got in the small cage and were wound down the shaft.

Bryn was surprised to find they were so cramped in the cage, but he realised that it was only meant for such an emergency operation as he was now embarking upon. He could feel the tension in the men and smell their fear in the confined space. Then suddenly as the cage descended towards whatever disaster they would find, the men broke into a deep vibrant singing—"O Iesu mawr, rho d'anian bur . . ." "Great Jesus, grant your pure grace . . . strengthen my feeble steps . . . ." Bryn realised that they sang, not because he, their conductor was with them, but because it was what they did naturally in any extremity—they sang. Sang In moving, wonderful harmony together.

By the time the cage had reached the foot of the shaft, Bryn was astonished to find that his fear had left him, his spirits had been peculiarly lifted, as had the mood of all the men who poured out of the cage into the dark, oppressive and smoke-filled atmosphere of the level. His career as choir conductor had afforded him all kinds of musical experiences, but this singing he had just heard was different. This was new. This was for real. This was music communicating strength and confidence and hope to these men, helping them to suppress and overcome the fear and horror of their immediate situation and surroundings.

As they struggled through the darkness towards the roof-fall which they knew had converted the work-place of No.5 seam into a frightening prison, their safety lamps dimly showed up charred and still-smouldering pit-props and broken trams, which had been blown off their rails by the blast of dust and flames careering down the confines of the tunnel. In the corner, near the entrance to No.5 seam, they saw the burnt bodies of three pit-ponies, a gruesome warning of the human bodies they might yet find behind the roof-fall they were now preparing to clear. Beside the three bodies stood another pony, sad and forlorn and only partly charred, but amazingly, still alive. He had been sheltered from the blistering heat of the rush of flames, by the bodies of his confederates. Such were the vagaries of pit explosions and their associated flash flames.

"Look!" Exclaimed Bill suddenly, "See that big rock right in the corner of the face of the fall, if we can move him, it'll give us a good start to getting through."

"We'll never shift that one, Bill, it's too heavy," replied one of the rescuers.

"Oh yes we will. We can use the pony. Quick rope him up to the rock."

The men set to, tying one of the ropes they had brought with them around the shoulders of the pony and looping the other end round a convenient protuberance at the top of the rock, which was nearly as tall as they were.

"Right," ordered Bill, "Some of you grab the rope and pull with the pony. NOW PULL!" Men and animal strove against the weight of the rock, lodged under the front of the fall. Suddenly it gave way, tumbling out from the rest of the rocks and bringing a rush of smaller ones with it. The men cheered at their success.

"Well done lads, we must take that pony back up with us and retire him early! Now look, that's the escape hole started. Keep it tight to that right hand corner, the rock's looser there. We'll need to prop it as we go."

They started to attack the rock face with picks and crow-bars, shovelling the loosened stones back out of their way. The tunnel was small, about two foot square, and as they progressed, foot by foot, they forced shortened pit-props under the rough ceiling. They dug, one at a time, lying on their stomachs as the escape tunnel forced its way through the rockfall. It was difficult, awkward work, but they stuck at it energetically until they were almost two yards into the fall of rock and knew from their past experience that they were nearly through. They soon would know the fate of their friends.

Bill Pritchard said authoritatively, "O.K. boyos. I'll finish her off. My Harry's in there and I want to be the one to get to him first." With that, the man whose turn it had been to dig, crawled backwards out of the tiny tunnel and Bill squeezed his way in instead of him, flat on his stomach towards his trapped son, wondering what disaster he might find in the seam ahead.

## Chapter 17
# Buried

Harry, and his friend Idwal, as the juniors of the gang, had been taking their early morning break in a small crevice-like shelter that they had left in the wall of the tunnel of No.5 seam. In it there was a convenient flat rock to sit on, and right next to it, a very large upright rock that the miners had decided to tunnel around because of it size, leaving it sticking out from the wall of the tunnel, It was that rock that formed the crevice. The boys had got used to leaning their aching backs up against it in their breaks, facing backwards down and away from the face of the tunnel, drinking their tea and munching their sandwiches, both laced with copious amounts of black coal-dust.

It was also that rock that saved them when one of the workers up at the face threw the faulty electric switch that ignited the lethal mixture of marsh-gas, air and coal-dust, and caused the first explosion, to fire a massive blast of flame down the narrow tunnel, into the wider levels that linked the coal seams, and on

*Strange Harmony*

into the rest of the mine-workings one thousand feet below the surface.

The explosion, and the two that closely followed it, shook the layers of rock and coal and earth of the mine and the surrounding area like an earthquake. That is what it felt like far away in the village. But the shaking the village received was nothing to the disaster that overcame anything or anyone in the vicinity of the explosions and in the path of the fire.

The ball of fire that tore through the mine from that first tiny spark, burnt up everything in its path: pit-props and timbers that held up the roof, all combustible equipment lying around, and tragically, any men and pit-ponies that it hit.

Luckily for the boys, the huge, up-right rock that had been their back-rest was blown over by the enormous blast, falling across them and sheltering them from the rushing flames that had momentarily filled the coal-face face and then had careered on down the seam and away from them into the main mine-workings.

"Iddy, are you all right?" asked Harry, tremulously.

"Except for my chest, Harry." Came the subdued answer. "At least I can move a bit. The end of this here massive rock got propped up by the rock we were sitting on, otherwise I'd have been flattened! We'd better get out from it quick."

"O.K. I can just about move my body. Can't feel my legs though. They seem stuck under the end of the rock when it hit the ground. Can you see anything, Iddy boy? It's awful dark."

"I'll try to crawl out from under here. I can see a lamp still lit up towards the face. I think I can get it."

"Good boy, Iddy. Go and get it and then pull me out of here."

Idwal crawled painfully up to the face of the seam.

"Harry!" He said, almost whispering, pain and fear cracking his voice, "They're all dead . . . . Burnt to bits. Clothes an' all." Young Idwal, on his hands and knees and holding the single safety lamp, stared in horror at the burnt bodies of the five men who, minutes before, had been members of their gang. "Oh, Harry it's awful. And my chest is beginning to hurt something terrible."

"Come back here, Iddy boy, and get me free of this rock. Then we can see about getting out."

Idwal, face white with shock and eyes full of tears, crawled back to his friend who was trying to wriggle his legs out from under the rock. He put his arms under Harry's armpits and tugged. They pulled and struggled until Harry's legs worked free of the rock. Both the boys lay back panting in the gravel and dust of the tunnel and stayed where they were for some while, both weak from their ordeal.

After a while Harry said quietly

"My legs look a funny shape, Iddy, and I still can't feel them."

*Strange Harmony*

"I think they're broken, butty. Just lie there quiet a minute. We're both crocked. I think. My chest is getting worse—it's hard to breathe"

"That's just because the entrance to the seam is blocked by that fall there, and there's no air coming in," replied Harry.

For the first time since the blast, Idwal looked down the tunnel and saw the solid face of rough rock filling the whole of the entrance. His eyes widened and his voice broke as he said,

"That . . . means . . . . we're buried . . . . Harry . . . and . . . we'll never get out . . . again."

The little boy began to sob uncontrollably.

"It's all right, Iddy. They'll get us out, don't you worry. My Dad says miners 'ave got to be made of steel. He'll come for us, I know. So cheer up, they'll be here soon."

The boys lay back and waited for what seemed to them an eternity. Then Idwal lifted his head from the stone floor,

"Harry what's that noise? Seems to be in that corner of the fall."

They both held their breath and listened intently.

"Yes Id. It's them! I TOLD YOU MY DAD WOULD COME!"

Harry cheered excitedly as he saw the rocks at the bottom of the solid wall fall away and a hole appear in it, about one foot round. And then, through the hole appeared the coal-blackened face of his beloved Dad.

"Thank God Harry! I knew you were alive. "Bill Pritchard whispered fervently as he saw his son. "Come on boy, we can go home now."

"Harry's broken his legs, Mr. Pritchard, he can't move. And the others are dead, and my chest is crushed in . . . ."

"Hold on then, Idwal. Crawl over here boy, lie on your back and I'll pull you through the hole we've dug. I can't come through any further your side. I don't think the roof's going to hold if I move much more. That's it. It's a bit of a squeeze, but it's only for a couple of yards."

Bill caught hold of the boy's arms, pulled him into the tiny hole he was lying in and eased him past his body through towards the men the other side of the fall.

"Now then Harry my son, come and do the same as Idwal. Crawl to me." Bill encouraged his eldest boy to reach his hands. "That's my boyo. Give me your hands and I'll pull you past me to the others. As quick as you can now!"

"Thanks Dad. I'm nearly through."

Bill could feel the roof above his back creaking as he gently pushed his son underneath and past his own body to the rescuers waiting beyond his feet which still stuck out of the end of the small tunnel they had dug through the roof-fall.

"Well done, Bill. We've got him" Bryn said exultantly, "Now then, we'll pull you back out. Hang on . . . ."

Suddenly there was a great cracking sound. The short props holding up the roof of the escape tunnel gave way and tens of tons of rock fell into it, crushing Bill's body into the stony floor he was lying on.

"NO! NO! Daa . . . ad" Harry's voice faded out in horror as he saw the rocks bury his father and seal him into the new fall.

Bryn stared at the fallen rocks, caught hold of the boy and sobbed impotently "Bill—NO! Not you!"

The rescue party stood in horrified silence as they saw Bill's feet twitch briefly and then become ominously still. They gently put the two boys on stretchers and carried them to the cage.

On its slow upward journey, because of the stretchers, the cage was even more confined than when it had descended into the depths of the mine. Instead of feeling relieved that they were on the way to the surface and to fresh air and freedom, Bryn felt a deep, deep sadness pressing in on him. Suddenly, the rescuers began to sing again—"Dyma gariad fel y moroedd . . . ." "Here's a love deep as the ocean." As before, the singing strangely lifted his spirits. He looked at the broken body of young Harry and thought of Bill, his friend, and what he had done to save his son. A great wave of sadness and admiration flowed through him as he looked at the men of the rescue party, singing so movingly around him, tears streaming down their faces and leaving white rivulets through the night-black coal-dust that covered them.

# Chapter 18
# The Investigation Begins

Karen Thomas became extremely alarmed when she heard the news that her father, who had started the riot at the opening of the railway line, had escaped from prison. She looked with concern at her sister, Hannah Pritchard who she had come to support at the pit-head on the morning of the explosion, and said

"I know you've got plenty to worry about with your William and the boys, but I'm really worried about Dad. If he's got out, the first thing he'll do is go for Ray Roberts. You know he said he'd kill him after he was arrested. And Ray is very vulnerable now with all this investigation business starting again because of the accident. I hope Dad doesn't do anything silly."

"Yes, you're right, Karen. But the thought of Harry and William trapped down there in that inferno is more than enough for me just now. Dad will have to look after himself. I've got to stay here"

Hannah and the other women of the village had seen the rescue teams arrive from the new Rescue Centre, which had only recently been set up as a result of the

*Strange Harmony*

Mines Act, passed just a couple of years before. Even in their consternation and anxiety they had been very impressed by the efficient way the teams had clicked into their rescue procedures: very different from the chaos of five years ago, after the first explosion they'd had down the mine.

The engineers had got the cage and its hoisting machinery working again and had already brought up one crowd of shaken, relieved men. Their women had been equally relieved to welcome them to the surface, many of them unhurt. However, the rest of the women still stood around the yard, tense and anxious, waiting for news of their own husbands and sons and brothers.

Young Jim had returned, with the other rescued men from the north shaft, to be hugged joyfully by his mother. He told her his exciting story,

"Dad got me out, Mam, and then he went back for Harry. I hope they're all right. It's awful down there, Mam. Dad was burnt on his face."

"They'll be all right, son. You come and help me finish bandaging these men, then we'll go and meet your Dad and Harry after that."

Hannah had been helping Phoebe and Dr. Morgan and the first-aiders in the make-shift hospital they had set up in the changing room. She couldn't help noticing all the safety inspectors who were going around interviewing the men who had been brought to the surface. That was another change brought about by the Act: this time the accident would be properly investigated and Roberts would have to answer to the Court of Enquiry that would be bound to follow.

When Ray Roberts came back to the main shaft with little Jim and the others, he was immediately approached by two inspectors who had been talking to Haydn Morgan, the mine's own safety engineer. Hannah noticed how white Robert's face became as he argued loudly and vehemently with the inspectors. He was remonstrating with Haydn Morgan, and gesticulating wildly about something Morgan had said.

Hannah could guess what was happening, because her William had told her about the on-going battle between Roberts and his safety engineer, and had described all the obstacles the management and owners of the mine had put up to delay the introduction of the new safety measures which the Act demanded.

She could imagine how alarmed Roberts was at the thought of being found guilty of negligence again; especially that now it had been made a criminal offence and a prison sentence would inevitably follow under the new Act. No wonder he was blustering angrily in front of the inspectors.

She finished helping to put a splint on the broken leg of the man her team was attending and said to

Jim and Karen, trying to look as though she wasn't worried, but failing abysmally,

"Come on then, you two. Let's go and see how William and Harry are doing."

And off they walked, over the fields to the north shaft.

As they approached the yard surrounding the mineshaft they saw an ambulance speed up to it. Hannah's heart lurched, but she had no time to think any further, for the men around the shaft gave a cheer as the ascending cage came to a halt and the doors clanged open.

Seven men, covered in grime and coal-dust, carried two stretchers out from the cage. Hannah's hands flew to her face and her eyes opened wide with fear, as on the nearest stretcher she saw her eldest son, Harry, both his legs tied up with rough, temporary splints and bandages. She ran to his side and cried out

"Oh my Harry! What have you done?"

"I haven't done nothin', Mam." Harry replied, "The rocks just fell on my legs and broke them. Me and Idwal were buried for a bit. But I'm O.K. now. Dad got us out, but I'm worried about him, Mam. He's still down there."

The men had obviously not told the boy about his father's death. Hannah looked terrified now,

"Bryn!" She cried as she saw the conductor by the stretcher. "Where's my William? WHAT'S HAPPENED TO HIM?"

"Come and sit over by me, Hannah." Said Bryn gravely.

"NO! I DON'T WANT TO SIT. Just tell me what's happened to my William!"

"I am afraid he's dead, Hannah." Bryn added quietly, "He died saving Harry. He was amazing Hannah. Strong as steel, as he always used to stay."

The woman's face went ashen white, but no tears fell from her eyes.

"Well that's it then. Somehow I'd been expecting this. Well, go with God, William. Come on Harry, let's get you to hospital and then we can go home again. You're head of the family now, my little man."

The boy struggled to fight back his own tears when he saw his mother receive the awful news of her husband. He grasped her hand tightly,

"Yes, I know, Mam. But we'll be all right. We'll be all right."

Bryn looked with admiration and astonishment at the two brave figures in the ambulance, while Karen, noticing his reaction, said,

"They will, too. The faith of that family is amazing. They are all so strong."

Bryn looked at her and then at Hannah, and replied,

"Yes. I see what you mean."

However, for himself, he felt totally bereft at the loss of his best friend so, he turned away, filthy, and covered in coal-dust, to walk back to the main yard to see if he could get a shower and borrow some clean clothes.

When he got back to the main shaft he saw that the mine owners had arrived at the scene of the explosion. With them stood the Chief Inspector who would be leading the official enquiry into the accident. They were talking to a group of local inspectors, and there in the middle of them was Haydn Morgan, the safety engineer, looking serious and worried, facing Roberts, whose face had turned purple with anger, as he defiantly defended himself in a loud voice, so that all the on-lookers could hear everything he said.

"You were supposed to be keeping the record sheets, Morgan!" He shouted.

"No. Mr. Roberts. That was your job. I trained the men who we selected to check the switches and the air quality, and I set up the systems for recording the results. *You* had the record sheets sent to your office for safe keeping."

"Well we'd better go to the bloody office to see if they're there then!"

"I sincerely hope they *are* there, Mr. Roberts." Said the Chief Inspector, with a frown on his face, "After all the other things I've heard from these men, we've clearly a lot of investigating to do. We'll need to find a date for the Enquiry, too. Sometime towards the end of next week, I would hope, when the Magistrate can be there to hear the result of our investigation."

Roberts blanched at this news of the Official Enquiry, as he could already guess the outcome. He turned sharply on his heel and led the small group of officials back to his office to look for the records.

# Chapter 19
# The Men Return

The rescue work continued for the rest of the week. The speed and efficiency of the newly formed rescue teams had fortunately cut down the number of deaths. So far, the only fatalities had been the six men who died when the cage of the main shaft was blown to the surface, the five who were burned in No.5 seam and one fifty three year old father of five who had worked in the mine for over forty years, and had suffered a heart attack at the coal-face where he was working. Many other miners had received injuries, mainly broken bones; some of the burns were frightening to behold, but none of these was found to be life-threatening.

The remaining able-bodied men were soon deployed, clearing up the debris the blast had left behind it and repairing burnt and broken pit-props and roof-timbers. All the miles of cables and sprinkler piping which had lain along them also had to be checked and replaced, as it was imperative to bring the mine back into production swiftly, to maintain profits for the owners and jobs for the villagers.

What was becoming patently clear to everyone was the mass of evidence that the inspectors were gathering about the cause of the accident, through their meticulous questioning of all the people involved, owners and workers. They had also collected a large variety of pieces of equipment together in the lamp-room, which their engineers were testing and analysing.

Everyone knew that the owners and Roberts, in particular, were in serious trouble. It could be seen clearly in the owners' faces as they walked around the mine, although Roberts himself had apparently been absent the last couple of days:

"Gone to America to escape prison, I expect!" Said one of the overmen, cynically. Other miners, angry at losing their friends in the accident, were much more seriously and openly critical of their mine manager.

With all this tension-filled activity going on, Bryn considered very seriously calling off the choir practice that had been scheduled for the end of the week.

He asked Phoebe what she thought they should do. She replied with unusual firmness,

"Bryn, you must carry on with the practice. After the trauma everyone's been through it'll do us all good. Making music is one of the best therapies."

"You're probably right, Phoebe, but I wish I could be as confident as you are about the deep healing effects of music. Maybe I will someday," responded Bryn.

"Maybe you will, one day." Her affection for him was clear.

"Phoebe, you are good for me, you know," said Bryn with a smile.

"I hope so, Bryn," answered the little accompanist, more than a little surprised at the unusual warmth she detected in the conductor's voice.

"I suppose it will be useful to keep on with the practice," he continued—"We've got some new music to prepare for the Swansea competition, so we need all the time we can get." He opened the music copies to explore with her how best to help the choir learn the new pieces, and his accompanist gratefully moved closer to him so that they could share the music more easily.

On the evening of the practice Bryn was surprised and delighted to see that the tenors and basses, missing from the choir ever since Ray Roberts had issued his ultimatum about their jobs because Bryn had missed his wife's funeral, had all turned up.

"Evening Bryn," "Glad to be back," "We've missed choir," they chorused as they entered the room.

"We've missed you too," responded Bryn, "Good to see you back. But aren't you still risking your jobs, coming to practice like this?"

*Alun Jones*

"Not anymore, boyo," answered Eifion James, one of the leading tenors,

"Roberts can't do anything to us now. He's on his way out himself, come the Enquiry. We're all going to visit him in Cardiff jail."

"Just to show him how much we love him!" Added Rod Evans, sarcastically, and the men laughed their approval of the jibe

"Well, welcome anyway," Bryn said, "Take your old places and we'll start. Phoebe's put copies of the new piece on your seats. It was composed by Hubert Parry just a few years ago. Remember, he also composed the anthem 'I was glad . . .' that we sang in our last competition." The members of the choir opened their copies, and listened closely to their conductor as he introduced the piece.

"It's a setting of an old, old poem by Henry Vaughan called 'My Soul'. Phoebe knows it well and says its wonderful, so I'll ask her to play it through for us to get the feel of it."

Phoebe played the piece beautifully because it was one of her favourite choir pieces. Her playing brought out the effect of the different rhythms of the four sections of the music and emphasised the varying dynamics that flowed through them. Most of the choir were well-experienced in reading the tonic sol-fa notation which they always used to learn their music. In the competition they would sing from memory without their copies, but a great deal of practising was ahead of them first, and for that they had Phoebe's piano-playing to help them learn to sing the music accurately.

"Right then," said Bryn, when Phoebe had completed the last triumphant chord, "You're all good readers. Let's just try it over—it's mainly a matter of getting hold of the changing rhythms, the notes are fairly straight forward."

He raised his baton, glanced at Phoebe, embraced the choir in one intense look of expectancy and brought them in exactly together with the first stirring chord of E minor: 'My Soul', they sang, and repeated it, 'My Soul'. The first time, the music resolved from the tonic E minor to its dominant chord, B major, but the second time, to its sub-dominant, A major. Bryn shivered inside himself, as he often did at the first few chords of any new piece. But for some reason, this was different. In both the resolved chords the basses sang the major third note, and not the more usual tonic of the chord, and that seemed to give the music a strange, ethereal quality. For Bryn, it wasn't the words they were singing that were affecting him, he was still far from convinced about the existence of souls anyway, rather, it was the whole effect of the interaction between the music and the words, combined with the fact that the whole choir was back together again after the mine disaster. A kind of wholeness that communicated itself through the singing. He knew he had not experienced such a thing before.

It immediately took him back to the time in the cage when the men had burst out singing in their fear and extremity. It was a similar powerful feeling he had had then. But the choir had gone on to sing the next section of the piece, '. . . There above noise and danger sweet peace sits crowned with smiles . . . .' they sang, and he was straightway transported back to that instant when eventually he had got out of the cage and had stepped into the fresh air, far above the noise and the danger and the darkness and the terror of the roof-fall they had dug the youngsters out of. And yes, he remembered, they *had* smiled, and a strange kind of peace *had* embraced him.

However, by then the choir had reached the next section and were singing in the comfortable key of G major, 'He is thy gracious friend . . . who did in pure love descend . . .' the face of Bill Pritchard appeared clearly before his eyes, He remembered vividly that moment when Bill had got back into the cage to descend into danger and darkness again, simply to save his son. Gracious friend, undoubtedly. Pure love, certainly. But the choir had completed the beautiful third section of music, with the chord of C major, the words of Henry Vaughan, 'to die here . . . . for thy sake,' ringing in his ears.

Again Bryn shivered deep inside and found himself so powerfully overcome by this insight from the seventeenth century, beautifully expressed by his choir and coming so close to his seeing Bill, gracious friend indeed, dying to save his son, that he almost broke down in tears in front of the singers. Instead he collected himself sternly, ignored the deep feelings he was experiencing and tapped his baton commandingly on the lectern in front of him, hoping his interruption would break the spell that the music had created.

"That was incredibly good for first sight, friends, I need to see if it was a one-off, so once again from the first bar," he said, unsteadily. "All right. Ready Phoebe?"

His interjection succeeded in breaking the strange link between his recent traumatic experiences down the mine and the beautiful piece his choir was learning. However, he was sure that something very deep indeed had moved him, and in some way, had changed him. When they started singing again, Bryn was much more his usual confidently technical self again, and they sang the piece through to its end. He then spent the rest of the practice taking the choir through the piece, bar by bar and section by section, analysing the music and explaining how he wanted each part interpreted.

When they all left the practice room together, Phoebe said,

"That was a very good practice, Bryn. I think you were inspired."

Bryn agreed with her. He had been unusually inspired. He knew the choir had made a great deal of progress, but he was much less certain about the progress he had made personally.

# Chapter 20
# Maggie's Confession

Karen and Maggie left the choir practice together. Karen looked at the attractive young girl walking next to her and said,

"What's the matter, Maggie? You're not your usual bubbly self this evening. The choir practice was O.K. wasn't it?"

"Oh yes the practice was good. I liked that new piece. It's just me. I'm a bit worried that's all," replied Maggie.

"Your Dad, is it?" Asked Karen. She knew that Maggie had problems with her father. Since her mother had died he had developed the habit of going missing for days on end, leaving Maggie alone, just waiting for him to turn up again. When he returned he would never say where he had been.

"Well yes, there's him. He's gone off again—yesterday I think it was. He'll be back again when he's ready. But it's not only him, there's other things. It would take a long time to tell you."

"It's Saturday tomorrow. Why don't you come over to my place in the evening and stay over a few days until he's back. We can have plenty of time to chat together then with nobody to disturb us."

"That would be nice, Karen. Thanks, I'd like that. See you tomorrow night, then." She waved to Karen as they reached the café with the flat above it, in the High Street, and carried on down to where she lived with her father further on down the road.

Karen waved back, feeling really sorry for the young girl.

Saturday evening, early, just as Karen was closing the café, Maggie turned up with a small bag,

"I've come for the night as you suggested. Where'll I put these? "She said.

"Good to see you. Take them up to box room, next to my bed-room. I've made the bed up there. It's quite comfortable. You'll be better here with me than on your own."

"Thanks, Karen." Maggie took her bag up the narrow stairs at the back of the café and grocery counter, to the tiny box room. "Oh it looks lovely. You've decorated it, haven't you?"

"Yes, and cleared all my junk out. It makes quite a nice bed-room now. Make yourself at home. We'll get some fish and chips for supper in a minute. Let's have a lemonade first, and relax a bit, then you can tell me what's worrying you."

Maggie took a deep breath and began,

"Well I suppose I might as well come straight out with it: I think I'm pregnant."

Karen's hands flew to her face with the shock. She cried out in alarm,

"Oh no, Maggie. Not you as well. Who was it?"

"It must have been my Uncle Ray . . . ."

"I knew it! I told you to watch him after he tried it on months ago. But are you sure you're pregnant?"

"I went to see Dr. Morgan, and he reckoned I definitely was. He said for me to come and see you actually. That's why I'm here."

"I'm glad you came, Maggie. You know it's terrible if it was your Uncle Ray. After what I'd told you too. What happened this time?"

"The week after that first time when he caught me on his bed and gave me that gin, he made some excuse about needing help to fix something in his bedroom, and like a fool I went up with him."

"Oh, NO! That was stupid," exclaimed Karen, "And then . . . .?"

"Then he suggested we had some gin again, so as I quite liked it the time before, I drank some with him. We just sat on the bed and had a nice chat about school and things."

"Typical. He's so clever at that sort of thing. He did the same thing with me when I was your age. What happened next?"

"I was quite enjoying myself I suppose, so we had some more gin and I began to feel light-headed."

"I'm not surprised . . . ."

"Then he said for me to lie back on the bed and I would be all right. So I did, and I did feel better. It was all quite exciting really, and I wasn't worried. Then he started stroking my forehead and then the back of my neck, and said I should try some more gin. I don't remember much after that."

"The rotten . . . ." Karen started to say what she thought of Roberts, but Maggie carried on in a soft, dreamy sort of voice,

"I vaguely remember him stopping stroking my neck and starting on my tummy, and then smoothing my legs. I remember thinking it was nice, but I didn't seem to be really there. It was all very hazy. The next thing I knew I was sitting in Uncle Ray's chair in the lounge and he was giving me coffee. I'd never had coffee before. Like the gin,." She giggled and looked at Karen wickedly.

"So you didn't really know what he did to you."

"Not really, though I sort of guessed what he must have done—my knickers were on backwards," the girl giggled again.

"Maggie! You're impossible. You know that means he raped you. Was that the only time he did it?"

"Well no, not actually. After that I knew what he wanted, and I was sorry for him, I suppose, Auntie Megan having died and all that. So when he came home early from work and I was there cleaning, we'd go up to his bedroom. I suppose I enjoyed it really. Most times anyway. But now look what's happened," the girl looked at her friend in dismay. Karen frowned and admonished her,

"You are a silly girl. A baby at sixteen will be no fun, I can tell you. Does Ray know about it?"

"No fear! . . . . I can't tell him, can I? I haven't told anyone 'cept you and Dr. Morgan."

"You've got to tell him. He'll have to give you money to look after the baby, if he's the father. We've got to face him with it now, or he'll get away with it again. He never gave me a penny after Ronald was born, He just kept well out of it, and he'll do the same again if we give him half a chance."

"But if we tell Uncle Ray, then my father will get to know, and he'll kick me out of the house straight away. I know he will."

"Yes, I expect he will." Karen knew very well what Maggie's father would think of it, and what he would do. She went on, putting her arm around the girl,

"You don't need to worry about that, you can stay here with me for as long as you like. I know exactly what you are going through. But right now we've got to go and see Ray Roberts and face him with what he's done. Come on get your coat on, its beginning to drizzle, you mustn't get too wet in your state."

Outside it was very dark and very wet. The two young women walked up the High Street and on up to houses at the top of the village. There was the odd street gas-light dimly lighting their way, but they had to tread carefully over the uneven surface of the road.

Ahead up the hill, they could see the lights of the big houses of the mine managers and the few other professional families of the village, each in its own grounds. Soon they came to Robert's grand house at the top of a small crescent. They saw immediately that there were no lights on in it. As they reached the bottom of the drive-way, Maggie saw two dark figures leave the house and hurry furtively, not down the drive, but across the darkened lawn to a side gate in the hedge surrounding the house. She stopped Karen with her hand and whispered,

"Karen! Who's that up by the house?"

"Maggie." Karen whispered back in total surprise, "I think that first one's my father. What on earth is *he* doing here? Quick, hide behind this tree. They mustn't see us"

"And that's Bryn with him, I'm sure. What's *he* doing here, too?"

*Strange Harmony*

There was one gas-lamp at end of the crescent and they could just make out the crouching figures of the two men as they went through the gate.

"They obviously don't want to be seen or they'd have come down the drive," said Karen, as she moved quietly out from behind the tree."

"But what *do* you think they've been doing?" Asked Maggie urgently,

"I can't imagine. Although I know what my father would *like* to do to Ray Roberts, if he had the chance. After what Ray's landed you with, I'd help him do it."

"And Bryn can't stand him either. Uncle Ray has been really awful to him. Karen? The house is very quiet . . . . And dark . . . . You don't think . . . ?

"No I don't think," Karen butted in firmly. She knew what a vivid imagination Maggie had, "Let's go and see if Ray is there."

They approached the front door to ring the bell. Maggie exclaimed hoarsely,

"Look Karen! IT'S OPEN!" Her eyes opened wide as she stepped inside.

"Don't go in, Maggie, it's black as pitch."

"It's all right Karen. I know it like the back of my hand. UNCLE RAY!" She called out into the darkness, "Uncle Ray. Are you there?"

An eery silence followed her call. She called again, louder. A long silence.

"He's not here, Karen. I wonder where he can be?"

"I think we'd better go. I don't like this one little bit. Come on Maggie, there's nothing we can do here."

The older woman took the lead and started back down the drive.

"Should we shut the door, do you think?" Maggie asked tremulously,

"You can, if you like. Just pull it."

The door shut with a bang and the women ran away down the dark drive.

## Chapter 21

# Suicide?

Jane and Bryan O'Reilly had emigrated to the expanding South Wales mine-fields to escape unemployment and famine in their home-land. Bryan found work as a navvy in the new mines that were being built in the area and Jane took on the job of secretary to Ray Roberts.

Her first task was to sort out the shambles the office systems had been allowed to get into. She found it quite a challenge, and she soon realised why Roberts had not kept his previous secretaries for very long. He obviously expected much more from them than merely secretarial duties; the last one, Jane thought, had clearly been selected more for her compliance than her competence in the office. She soon found that she had to be firm with her boss if she was going to get him to accept that she had no interest in anything other than acting as his secretary. She had been a little surprised that, eventually, he had learned to behave himself with her because he realised that she would not put up with his rather blatant sexual advances.

The O'Reillys had gone to the Catholic Church back in their home town. They had not publicized the fact since coming to live in the village and had found a ready welcome waiting for them in the Baptist chapel at the end of the High Street. Jane, particularly, had come to love the intense emotional sound of the four part harmonies the congregation sang, and found it very moving, compared with the rather un-inspiring unison singing of her home church.

Bryan and Jane had joined the choir, as they both had clear, melodious voices, albeit coloured by their soft, Irish brogue.

This particular Sunday morning they sat in their usual places at the front of the huge gallery of the plain, unadorned chapel. Jane noticed that Ray Roberts had not taken his usual place at the end of the front row of the basses. This did not concern her immediately because she knew, as did everyone else, about the quarrel between Ray and the conductor of the choir, and the fact that Roberts had forbidden the men who worked in the mine to attend the choir.

Nevertheless, her boss had not turned up at the office for the last two days, and she knew the intense strain he was under because the Official Enquiry was to be held in the coming week. And now he was not to be seen anywhere else in the morning's congregation. She became more and more worried as the service proceeded.

When the service was over she turned to Bryan anxiously,

"I'm really worried about Mr. Roberts. He's not been around for three days now, and he looked awful when I saw him last. Do you think . . . ."

"Have a word with Dr. Morgan then," Bryan interjected somewhat abruptly; he had never liked nor trusted his wife's boss.

"There's Dr. Morgan now, speaking to Aneurin Rhys," Jane replied.

Sergeant Rhys was the well-respected police presence in the village and was standing just outside the entrance of the chapel, towering over the little doctor, and talking to him rather animatedly. Jane approached them and asked,

"Good morning Dr. Morgan. Do you think we should do something about Mr Roberts? I haven't seen him in the office the last two days and he's never missed coming in before without ringing me. Now he's not here in chapel."

"Funny you say that, Jane, Aneurin and I were just talking about Ray. Maybe we'd better go to his place and find out if anything has happened. Come with us if you like."

Sergeant Rhys called two of his constables over and the little group walked up the hill towards Robert's house.

There they found everything oppressively quiet. One of the constables knocked the front door loudly. A typical policeman's knock. One! Two! Three!—Silence. Sergeant Rhys walked backwards onto the lawn to look up at the windows. He called out,

"Mr. Roberts. ARE YOU THERE?" Again silence.

"Go and have a look around the back, Dave," Rhys instructed one of his men, who ran quickly around the large house, and came back to the small group, shaking his head,

"Can't see nothin', sergeant," he reported.

"Right, in that case we'd better break the door in. Come on lads," commanded the sergeant.

With that the two constables produced a large log from the garden, charged the door with it, broke the lock and with a tremendous crash ended up in the hall-way.

"If he was sleeping, sure and he's awake now!" said Bryan in his sing-song, Irish brogue. They looked briefly in the down-stairs rooms, then the doctor asked urgently,

"Do you smell gas?"

"I think I do. Quick! Upstairs." Exclaimed the sergeant

The men rushed upstairs. Jane followed.

"The bedroom over there . . . ." The sergeant pointed and ran across the landing to a closed door. "It's locked!" He added. "BREAK IT DOWN!"

The constables complied and burst into the gas-filled room.

*Strange Harmony*

"Quick! Open the window! I'll turn the gas off!" "Dr. Morgan shouted, holding a handkerchief to his mouth and nose. There, on the carpet, up against the bedside cupboard, he saw the massive, crumpled form of Ray Roberts, white hair stained with blood from a great gash on his forehead.

"He's been dead sometime," proclaimed the doctor, feeling for Robert's pulse.

"Don't touch anything," ordered the sergeant loudly. On the bed-side cupboard he saw a key, presumably for the room, placed carefully in front of a picture of Robert's wife. He checked the key in the door. It fitted.

"Go and ring the station, Dave. See if the Inspector's still there." Dave ran downstairs and the sergeant continued,

"Look for note somewhere, Doc. It looks like suicide to me with that key put so tidily here inside the room, *and* by his wife's picture. He must have locked the door himself from inside and then turned the tap of the gas-fire on.

"There doesn't seem to be a note, sergeant," said Dr Morgan, looking around the room, "But look at this news-cutting. It's the report of the investigation of the explosion five-years ago, when Roberts was prosecuted and fined. It must have been preying on his mind, especially with the thoughts of the Enquiry ahead of him later this week."

"Enough to be tipping anyone over the edge, I reckon. Poor man," observed Bryan from the door-way, his arm around his shocked wife. They had stayed just outside the room watching the dramatic events unravelling in front of them.

The sergeant and the remaining constable inspected the room carefully, and just as they were finishing, the Inspector came up the stairs into the room.

"Well now. What have we got here?" He asked officiously.

"Pretty clear case of suicide, sir," the sergeant replied. "Door locked from inside; key by a picture of his wife; news-cutting by the side; and gas tap on. Everyone knows Mr Roberts has been in a bad way for days, worrying about the explosion and all those dead miners. Obvious, I think."

"But how about the gash on his head, sergeant? Could anyone have hit him?"

"No chance, sir. No one else in the room—they couldn't have got out if they had been."

"He may have changed his mind after putting the gas on, and tried to get out of bed to turn it off," exclaimed the doctor, "Then he fell and hit his head on the corner of the bed-side cupboard here, and failed to get back to the gas-tap."

"You're probably right, doctor. It certainly looks pretty conclusive to me. Good work, Sergeant Rhys." The Inspector drew himself up and added in an officious, formal tone,

"I'll let the coroner know if you are happy about our conclusion, Dr. Morgan. Makes it much easier for us, I suppose."

"It does that, sir. Nice and tidy this one. O.K. lads, we'll let the morgue know. They'll do the rest up here. Let's go."

The men went downstairs, Jane walking with them with tears in her eyes. She had become quite fond of her formidable boss.

## Chapter 22
# Suspicion?

Maggie watched the little group walk down the drive from Robert's house. She was standing with the small crowd of other worshippers who had seen the policemen and Dr. Morgan leave the chapel and had followed them at a distance, out of curiosity.

As Dr. Morgan passed her, she whispered hoarsely,

"Doctor, can I see you for a moment?"

"Yes, of course Maggie. How are you getting on?" He asked quietly as he left the group and walked over to the girl.

"Its not about me being pregnant I want to see you about. That's going fine, I think. It's about my Uncle Ray. You've just been to his place, and I need to know . . . ."

"Yes, I understand. I'm so sorry to have to tell you, Maggie, we've just found him dead in his bedroom. We think he must have killed himself, because he'd locked the bedroom door from inside and turned the gas on. Poor man, it was all the strain he was under."

*Strange Harmony*

"I guessed that might seem like that. But that's just what I need to talk to you about. I'm very worried and I must tell someone . . . ."

"Tell some one what, Maggie?"

"You said Uncle Ray's bedroom was locked from inside,"

"Yes?"

"Well I've got a key for it, so . . . ."

"YOU'VE GOT THE KEY! So you *could* have been there last night and let yourself out of the room, after you had . . . .?" The doctor began in astonishment. Maggie interrupted him,

"That's why I had to tell someone . . . ."

"But you didn't . . . . Maggie, did you? Tell me you weren't there in Ray's place last night."

"That's the trouble. I *was* there," the whole story came tumbling out.

"Me and Karen came to see Uncle Ray last night. Karen said I had to tell him about the baby. She thought he'd raped me . . . . She was awfully mad . . . . Thought we ought to do something about it . . . . When we got there it was all dark, and we called and called."

"You didn't go in the house though?" asked the doctor beginning to get quite alarmed at the girl's story.

"Well yes we did. The front door was open, see. But nobody answered."

"Open?" exclaimed the doctor. "How . . . .?"

"We couldn't understand it either. But we saw Bryn Griffiths and Huw Thomas in the garden as we got to the house. They left ever so quickly through the side-gate, because they might have seen us. We thought they'd left the door open."

"BRYN AND HUW THOMAS? This is getting worse," the doctor was really worried now,

"But Huw's in prison," he said.

"No. He's escaped. So Karen was really afraid when she saw him in Uncle Ray's because of what her father said he'd do to him after he was arrested."

"But *they* didn't have a key to Ray's bedroom, did they? So they couldn't have . . . ."

"Well that's what I don't know. You see Bryn had seen the key I'd pinched. I'd shown it to him. He told me to keep quite about it. Said it might come in useful!"

The doctor could imagine what the police would deduce from Maggie's story, and considered briefly what he should do about it. He could see all sorts of trouble ahead, so he decided to check a few things for himself first. He told the girl,

"Now look Maggie. All this could put a different light on things, but Ray pretty obviously committed suicide, so for goodness sake don't tell anyone else yet."

"Not even the police?"

"Especially not the police. They would start off a whole new investigation, and that would do no-one any good—so let's keep the whole thing to ourselves, all right? Promise?"

"Aw, thanks Dr. Morgan. That's what I hoped you would say. I knew I should come to you first. I'm much happier now that you know about it. I promise I'll not tell anyone."

The doctor left the girl to return to his surgery. All he had heard filled him with foreboding. He knew all the people involved only too well. The possibilities the story had un-earthed were obvious to him. Both men had more than enough reason to take revenge on Ray Roberts. The doctor considered what else could have happened: Bryn could have had the key copied or got another one like it, and as strong as Roberts undoubtedly was, he could have been overcome by the two men. They only had to knock him out, turn the gas on, put Robert's own key by the picture and leave him locked in the room, using the key Bryn had got hold of. Leaving the news-cutting by the picture would have been a very clever touch.

He realised the same method had been open to the two women, although the chances of them being able to overcome Roberts, he thought, were doubtful. On the other hand, he knew what real, intense anger was capable of, and both women had every reason to be angry with Roberts—whether that was enough motive for them to murder him, again he had his doubts. But it wasn't beyond the realms of possibility, he thought.

He also knew Roberts had antagonised many other people in the village. He remembered his own altercations, and those of his brother, with the overbearing, unpleasant manager of the mine. And then there was the whole business of the accident and all the men killed because of Robert's negligence. Their relatives had motive enough to get rid of Roberts too. He realised that this new information would stir up a hornets nest in the village. He felt that keeping quiet about Maggie's story was probably the best policy, but there was one thing he needed to check for his own peace of mind.

As he was passing Bryn's flat and studio on his way to the surgery he thought he should take the chance to hear his side of the story. He could hear Bryn's piano from the pavement outside the flat; he listened for a moment and decided from the standard of the playing, it was probably Bryn practising on his own, so he knocked on the front door.

"Hullo, Handel. Come on in." Bryn welcomed his friend into his little studio and sat on the stool by the grand-piano,

"Sit there. It's the only comfortable chair in the place," indicating a high-backed, winged chair opposite the piano,

"Bad business about Ray Roberts," he went on, "Suicide wasn't it? It's gone round the village like wild-fire?"

"Well the police think so. But I needed to talk to you about it. That's why I called in"

"Oh? What do you want to know?"

The doctor took a long breath and asked,

"Bryn, were you there in Robert's place last night?"

"Oh, they saw us did they? We saw two figures coming up the drive so we got out quick. We ran for the side-gate. Neither of us wanted to be seen at Ray's place."

"Neither of you? Who else was there, then?"

"Huw Thomas, believe it or not, and I could guess what he was there for. Me—I'd simply gone to try and persuade Ray to let his men come back to the choir—but Huw would have been after something quite different. I just happened to bump into him. Gave me a scare I can tell you."

"So you went to see him together did you?"

"We didn't get that far. The house was all quiet and dark. We weren't sure he was in, but when we saw the two people come up the drive we ran for it."

"And left the front door open?"

"Oh. No! Did we? That was stupid."

"Lucky for you, the two people were Karen and Maggie."

"KAREN AND MAGGIE? But what on earth were they doing there at that time of night?"

"They'd gone to tell Roberts that Maggie was pregnant with his baby. They were going to have it out with him"

"Pregnant with *his* baby. So *they* killed him. It wasn't suicide after all . . . . I'm not surprised. Karen hated the man and Maggie must have been pretty mad at him too. She must have used the key she'd pinched from Robert's other bedroom. The same key fitted all the rooms."

"And you knew that! If you had access to the key too it could also have been *you* who killed him, before Maggie and Karen got there. Both you and Huw Thomas had every reason to want to get rid of Roberts, now didn't you?"

Bryn looked straight at his friend, and said,

"I promise you, Handel, it wasn't us. We ran away almost as soon as we got there. We didn't get a chance to go up-stairs, and we certainly didn't see Roberts. And we *definitely* didn't kill him. You know I wouldn't do a thing like that, no matter how much I disliked the man."

"I believe you, Bryn, but you must admit it could look very suspicious. You and Huw and the two girls had the opportunity to kill Roberts last night, and all of you had plenty of motive, but it would be impossible to prove it one way or another. The police are convinced it was suicide so I think it best to leave it like that. I know that Maggie will not say anything and neither will I. That's best for us all, I think."

"Thanks, Handel. You're a good friend," said Bryn as the doctor left.

# Chapter 23
# Bryn Finds His Soul

Bryn felt good. He'd been feeling good for over three weeks since Ray Robert's funeral. It had been a huge affair; all the mine owners and local dignitaries had come to pay their respects, and most of the villagers and mine-workers had attended. The choir had sung 'Myfanwy' again, as they had in Megan's funeral only months before.

He could not have guessed how much more relaxed he felt now that Ray and Megan were not there to challenge and obstruct every new idea he brought to the choir. He realised, in retrospect, how much of a thorn in his side they had been. He saw now how their continual, abrasive antagonism had affected his conducting. He also felt that the quality of the choir's singing was improving, now that there was no longer disharmony in the relationships between the members. He remembered what Phoebe had told him about the way his relationship with the Roberts had been affecting the quality of their singing. He hadn't believed it then, but he did now, there was altogether more wholeness and cohesion in the music they made.

The other thing that had affected his general mood and well-being was the outcome of the Enquiry. He had not been looking forward to it because of his memories of Bill Pritchard and his other friends who had died in the explosion. He felt it might have churned up all his past negative emotions about Ray Roberts and the way he managed the mine, and the miners who worked for him.

As it transpired, the owners and the manager were fairly quickly found guilty of negligence on four charges under the Act of 1911. It was made clear in the Enquiry that, had Ray Roberts not died, he would have now been starting a lengthy sentence in Cardiff jail. The owners were harshly criticised, fined £500 and had to pay each family who had lost a wage-earner, between £150 and £300 compensation, depending on the number of his dependents.

The fact that Roberts could not locate the records of the required regular checks of the quality of the air, was considered serious enough, but when this was combined with the lack of reversible ventilation fans and critical failures in the water-sprinkler system necessary to keep the dust in the mine-workings dampened down, the Enquiry deemed that an accident had been waiting to happen.

One of the old, faulty switches, which the mine manager and owners had not yet replaced with newly designed safety switches, was enough literally to spark off the explosion. That particular serious act of negligence was found to be the cause of the accident, and thereafter the law took its course.

Bryn was surprised to find that the cold efficiency of the legal processes that had been followed over the past weeks had had a peculiar cathartic effect on him, and that, too, had added to the buoyancy of his mood.

However, the thing that lifted his spirits most was the growing closeness of his relationship with Phoebe. He was beginning to feel quite differently about her as they worked together to prepare the choir for the coming competition. He was also convinced that the choir's singing was improving rapidly through the two practices they now held every week, especially as they were back up to strength again. He was looking forward to the competition with unusual excitement.

It seemed to Bryn that the evening of the competition came very quickly. The choir looked resplendent in their uniforms: black jackets and light blue, striped ties for the men, and black dresses for the women, with light blue sashes to match the men's ties. When he took over the choir one of the things he had insisted upon was that they should present themselves professionally. Hence the uniforms, all paid for by the proceeds of their many concerts. He smiled to see that some of the members looked quite nervous as they sat in the packed auditorium and listened to the first four choirs sing their pieces.

The atmosphere was electric; Bryn could feel the tension in the other competitors and had to admit to himself that their music was magnificent. At the end of the fourth choir's performance, he whispered encouragingly to Phoebe next to him,

"They're good. But we can do better than that."

"We can, but we'll have to sing with all our souls," she answered pointedly.

Bryn smiled at her fondly,

"Let's go," he said, and the choir walked calmly to the stage and took up their positions. The crowd was hushed. The members of the choir drew themselves up, backs straight, feet together, as Bryn had taught them, and looked around the audience confidently. They were ready.

Bryn raised his baton. Phoebe, looking at him intently, played a quiet chord of E minor on the Bechstein grand piano at her finger-tips, and conductor, accompanist and choir began as one: 'My soul', they sang quietly, with a clear intensity. And again, 'My soul', this second time with a beautifully smooth crescendo, then swiftly back almost to a whisper—'there is a country far beyond the stars . . . .' they sang, again with another crescendo. That was a superb start, thought Bryn, proudly, he knew how

*Alun Jones*

important smooth, marked dynamics, quiet singing to loud and back again, were to most adjudicators.

He had no time to think, however, a change of key to a bright D major had taken the choir into the next section, a quiet, dainty, dance-like tune, now in six-eight time. And suddenly there it was again, '. . . . above noise and danger, sweet peace sits crowned with smiles . . . .' they sang, and all the deep feelings he had experienced in the rescue attempt came flooding back. He pushed them away swiftly. He could not afford to lose his concentration at this point. Luckily he knew, that, by this stage of the singing, he was conducting almost automatically.

Then, smoothly, they were into the next section, back to the key of G major—'. . . . he is thy gracious friend . . .' the choir's singing expressed movingly the deep compassion the poet's words were struggling to convey, and the faces of his friend Bill and his beloved son, Harry, swam into his mind again. He pushed them away, concentrating hard, because the choir was negotiating a demanding modulation into G minor. Bryn shivered, mouthing the words of the seventeenth century poet which his choir was singing so unerringly—'O, my soul awake!'—they burst, double forte, into that final imperative syllable with an unusually arresting change of key to E flat major.

Bryn was thrilled. Suddenly it dawned on him what was happening. Normally, when conducting, he felt totally focussed and almost aggressively competitive. In charge of the choir, in front of the choir, but definitely apart from the choir. Outside it all, controlling it. He was the master musician, playing the choir like complex instrument. But this time a strange, strong sense of wholeness and completeness came over him. *Took* him over, in fact. It was as though he and the choir were performing in perfect partnership. They, together, had *entered into* the music and were being swept along by it in perfect harmony.

Bryn knew he had not experienced anything like it before in the whole of his conducting career. The music they were making was more vivid and intense than he had ever known. He was conscious of feeling excited and totally at peace at the same time. He was sure he had discovered his own 'flower of peace', the same flower that Henry Vaughan had seen in his poet's eye so many years before; the same deep feeling that his choir was re-creating, as they sang Parry's glorious music. And, at that moment, he became certain that they were going to win.

More important, he was amazed to admit to himself, he knew that he and his choir were making the most wonderful music he had ever experienced. Perhaps he had found the soul that his Phoebe had gently suggested he had let shrivel up.

The applause that burst from the audience at the end of their singing was tumultuous. The choir bowed to the audience, while Bryn stood aside, acknowledging their achievement. The adjudicators were even more impressed than the audience and, in offering their verdict, struggled to find adjectives to describe the quality of the performance. Two of them confessed to having shed tears, as they quoted movingly 'at the way the choir was able to evoke such a thrilling mixture of joy and grief in the same piece of music.'

Bryn accepted the cup from the Chairman of the adjudicating panel, and, calmly, and with great dignity, presented it to the members of his choir who, still jumping up and down with excitement, proudly passed it around from hand to hand, to the continuing noise of cheering and hand-clapping. It was a wonderful moment for them all, and Phoebe surpassed herself as, bursting with admiration, she ran to Bryn and enveloped him in a great hug and kissed him, right there in front of the choir.

Bryn responded warmly, surprisingly free from embarrassment. He found he had difficulty admitting to himself which he valued most: finding his soul which, he was convinced, in future would transform his music, or discovering Phoebe's real, deep affection, perhaps her love for him, which he was pretty certain would change his life.

# Chapter 24
# Phoebe And Bryn

Phoebe looked at her father with affection and sadness in her blue eyes. She was sitting at his bedside in the desperately depressing geriatric ward of the County Hospital, just quietly holding his hand.

"He'll be quiet for a bit now," said the Staff Nurse softly. She had attended to her patient swiftly when he had become agitated again, fighting for breath, as he had been all the previous night. Phoebe had seen it all before when she had helped nurse other patients, but this was her Dad. This was different. She felt a part of the suffering he had been going through for three days, trying to share it with him.

She sighed, tears beginning to form again in her eyes. Her Dad had always had breathing difficulties following his forty years working down the mine; years of breathing coal-dust and often foul air, but he always made light of his infirmity protesting that he was pretty good for his age.

She had looked after him lovingly since her mother had died, four years ago. Her father always said that the loss of her remaining two brothers, killed in the pit explosion five years back, had ended her mother's interest in living. He had quietly and stoically struggled on after he'd lost her. Three days ago he had gone down with pneumonia after getting cold and wet on one of his regular walks. Dr. Handel Morgan had immediately taken him into the hospital., and now, to Phoebe's professional eye, her father's condition was deteriorating rapidly.

The Staff Nurse confirmed her diagnosis, as she put her hand on Phoebe's shoulder and said,

"I am afraid he's very sick, Phoebe. I think you ought to prepare yourself for the worst. It's such a shame, he was doing so well before this, wasn't he?"

"Yes," answered Phoebe, "He's done very well since mum died, but it affected him badly, really. He just didn't want to show it, you know what these miners are like. I suppose he had something like this coming to him after years in the pit."

She looked around the ward at the other ex-miners lying there, all of them fighting for breath and none of them yet fifty years old. She'd always hated the mine for what it had done to her father and all his friends, but she knew they had had no alternative means of employment in the valley; there had been no chance for them to support their families in any other way.

She glanced at her father again and shook her head sadly. In one way she felt glad that her mother was not there to see him suffer; she knew she would have been inconsolable. Phoebe smiled to herself, as she realised that her mum would at least have been happy with the sheets and pillows on all the beds. They were immaculate, just as her own had always been in her home. Different from their home though, Phoebe thought wistfully, the hospital obviously put cleanliness before comfort. She looked around at the plain, sparsely furnished ward and sighed again. If she had been in charge she would have tried to make it a little more welcoming and homely, but she knew how short of money the hospital always was. If it hadn't been for the support of the Miners' Union, it probably wouldn't have been able to remain open at all.

The ward was quiet now except for an occasional rasping breath as her father stirred in his sleep and tried to clear his dust-lined lungs. She turned and noticed a dark figure standing quietly at the door of the ward. She beckoned the figure over to where she sat in the dimly-lit ward, and then felt a thrill of anticipation as she realised that it was Bryn.

"I'd heard your father had been brought into hospital. I thought you'd be on your own at this time of night and you might want some company," he said.

"Oh, Bryn. There's kind of you." Her eyes filled with tears as she stood to welcome him. There was no one she would rather have with her at this trying time than her conductor and friend.

Bryn put his arm around her shoulders in a natural, friendly, compassionate gesture. She shivered a little, surprised by the feeling of excited anticipation his closeness and sympathy evoked in her: in all the times they had been alone together in his studio no sexual signal or innuendo had ever passed between them. Music had been the only motive behind, and the sole professional focus of their relationship so far. But Phoebe had become acutely aware of a growing warmth and closeness in many of Bryn's responses to her recently, and something, long dormant inside her, now stirred at his touch.

In her own current special need of love, she moved closer within his embrace and said,

"It's so good of you to be here. It probably won't be long now."

"I'm so sorry it's come to this," Bryn responded gently, "Your father seemed to be doing so well, I thought he'd go on for ever, the way you were looking after him."

"It's all right Bryn. Thanks. Yes, he has been fine with me, but since mother died, with the boys gone, he's not really been here with us. Understandable really. It'll be a happy release for him to be with her again."

"You are amazing. You really believe that don't you?"

"Yes I do. I've got to, to make sense of things. I wish you did."

"I know you do, but I just can't. Not since my parents died."

*Strange Harmony*

"Well it would help . . . . you know . . . . if you could bring yourself to believe . . ."

She hesitated, knowing this was a sensitive topic between them,

"Phoebe. You are a treasure. You are good for me—just as you were for your parents." Bryn drew his breath in sharply as he realised he had used the past tense for both her parents. She picked up his embarrassment immediately,

"It's all right, Bryn, it really is. Dad's nearly gone, and he's not in any pain now." She was partly in her nurses' role now, it was her best defence,

"That's the important thing," she went on, "He doesn't know what's happening to him anymore." She picked up her father's limp hand and held it tightly.

Then they both looked around in surprise as Dr. Handel Morgan walked quietly into the ward.

"Hullo, you two. I thought I might find you here, Bryn. You know I always thought you two were made for each other. How's Dad, Phoebe? Quiet, now?"

"Yes, he's peaceful now. Thank you, doctor." She was just a little embarrassed to hear his comment about her and Bryn, but deep down, pleased to discover what the doctor thought about their relationship.

"Thank you so much for coming back again, after all you did for father. I'm very grateful."

"Not at all. I've always been very fond of the old boy, and I've admired him too, the way he's coped since Susan died."

"Well thanks anyway. I appreciate it."

"And you're not so bad either, Nurse Phoebe," he said, with a wink at Bryn.

"You're always caring for other people, it's about time someone looked after you." The doctor looked meaningfully at Bryn.

"I agree," said Bryn, with such a depth of feeling that Phoebe glanced at him questioningly, but the moment passed as Phoebe's father let out a long sigh and his cold hand fell, lifeless, out of his daughter's warm grasp.

"Bless him," said Phoebe fervently, "He's gone. Go with God, Dad."

"Amen," said Bryn surprising himself with this automatic response, and putting his arm around Phoebe once more.

"There. It's all right now Phoebe. He's at peace," said the doctor, who smiled as he saw Phoebe respond to Bryn's embrace with the slightest of sobs. Bryn knew the doctor was a believer as well as Phoebe, and felt humble as he saw the response of both of these two friends to the old miner's death.

He was affected even more as Phoebe stopped crying, took up her father's cold hand and began to sing a verse of a Welsh funeral hymn, 'Rho im yr hedd . . . .' 'Give me the peace that's beyond my understanding . . . .' Bryn looked at the grieving woman in amazement as he saw in her face and heard in her singing, the same 'sweet peace ' that Henry Vaughan had felt and written about, two hundred and fifty years earlier, and which the choir had tried to express in the recent competition.

In that flash of insight he also saw how important it was to the poet that others should be helped to discover that place of peace—'If thou canst get but thither . . . .' and at the same time he understood why Phoebe had been trying to help him reach it too. He wished with all his heart that, some day, he might learn how to get there. He only knew, as he struggled with his own tangled emotions, that he wasn't there yet, and this was amply confirmed for him as he observed with wonder, the two calm, peaceful people at his side.

"I'll go and tell the Staff Nurse," said the doctor quietly, "You two stay there for a while. It'll do you good," and with that he left them together and walked out of the ward to find the nurse.

# Chapter 25
# The Roberts' Educaton Trust

Bryn was ecstatic. Two bits of good news in one day was too much to hope for, especially after the trauma of Phoebe's father's death. That morning, in his first post, he found a letter headed by an important looking crest. It was from an impresario who apparently had heard his choir in the Swansea competition when they had won with so much acclaim from the adjudicators and the audience. The impresario, likewise, had been very impressed, and in his letter he was inviting Bryn and his choir to take part in an international concert of top choirs in the Albert Hall. Bryn accepted the invitation with alacrity, delighted to think that he had at last received the recognition he had been seeking.

On top of that accolade, he had also heard that he was being offered the Assistant Organist's job at the cathedral. The news of this further success thrilled him, especially the thought of gaining access to the magnificent cathedral organ and all the wonderful music that that would open up before him. He confessed to Phoebe,

*Strange Harmony*

"It's not just getting the job. I'd been hoping I might be able to do that, but it's all that amazing cathedral music that I can now get involved in. It's just hit me."

Phoebe couldn't miss the chance, so with an admiring smile she added,

"Just think how much good that'll do to your soul!"

"Trust you to bring that up, but yes, I agree with you." He responded positively to her banter, because he now knew what she meant by it.

"But, seriously, Bryn, playing at the cathedral won't mean you'll be taken away from the village too much, will it? You'll still be able to lead the choir?"

"Of courses I will! I wouldn't have taken the job if it meant moving away from the village. I'll just need to travel to Cardiff sometimes in the week and on Sundays of course. I'll use the train. It'll be easy."

"Well I hope you won't overdo it . . . ."

"Oh, Phoebe, don't mother me. It's a great opportunity. It'll be fine."

"Good. I'm very proud of you. I'm sure you'll do well, and I know it's just what you wanted. Better than teaching at the school."

"Well, yes. But there'll be plenty of room for teaching at the cathedral too. It'll just be different that's all."

As the weeks passed, Bryn began to think that everything in his life was different. The choir won two more competitions. Granted they were quite small, local ones, but they were good experience for the choir as he pursued his ambition of National recognition for them. What was more important, Bryn knew that the quality of their singing was improving markedly, month by month, and he was preparing them for the concert in the Albert Hall with more than his usual enthusiasm.

The village was different too. As he had experienced at first hand in the rescue teams, disaster and danger and tragedy had the potential of releasing an amazing extent of compassion and comradeship and generosity, and this had happened in abundance amongst the people of the community. Families who had lost their principal wage-earners were being supported financially and practically by hosts of neighbours, friends and relations. There was great deprivation as a result of the explosion and consequent deaths, but the village overflowed with mutual concern and caring. After the immediate horror of the explosion the reaction of the people changed from a shocked paralysis to a proud and courageous facing of the new circumstances they had been plunged into.

Bryn could see clearly that the grief they suffered was profound, but that their faith and courage and determination helped them overcome it. The thing that impressed and affected him most was the way the people appeared to be able to gain strength from each other. This offered him a mirror to see in a new light what was happening between Phoebe and himself, for he realised he had changed at least as much as any of the villagers.

However, it felt to him as if he were on a very rough sea voyage, one minute elated and riding on top of waves of success, the next devastated and in the depths of despair about a friend's death or some other tragedy. He was aware of deep-lying feelings of insecurity. The peace he had felt at Phoebe's father's bedside had been short-lived, because, he now realised, he had not yet found the kind of stable foundation for his life that she had for hers. In a strange way, his recent successes had seemed to have added to his feelings of insecurity.

The words of the choir's competition piece that had so affected him before, came into his mind '. . . . none shall thee secure, but one who never changes.' Henry Vaughan had discovered it, as well as Phoebe, and probably Hannah Pritchard and many of the bereaved women of the village too. They were obviously coping with life's mixture of life and death, joy and sadness, elation and despair much better than he was.

About a week after he had heard about the invitation and his cathedral appointment he received a message from the solicitors in the village inviting him to attend a meeting with George Evans, the senior partner, at his office. Phoebe had received a similar invitation, so they walked to the solicitors' office together.

When they arrived they saw that Dr. Handel Morgan was already sitting in the office, talking to Mr. Evans, who welcomed them formally but warmly, to sit with them round the highly polished oak table in the middle of the room.

"Please come in and make yourself at home. You'll all be wondering what this is about?" They nodded,

"Well I've invited you here to ask you if you would all be willing to act as the Trustees of the Roberts' Education Fund."

"The Robert's Education Fund?" Queried Bryn.

"It's not widely known yet, but Ray and Megan Roberts left most of their estate in Trust for the education of musically gifted children of the village, to finance their further study of music at university or college."

"That's wonderful," exclaimed Phoebe, "how generous of them."

"They had no children or other close relatives left living, and as they both loved music, and choir singing in particular, this is obviously what they wanted to do with their money. They talked it over with me even before Megan died."

Bryn looked at the solicitor with some embarrassment,

"That's very good news, but they wouldn't have wanted me as a Trustee, I am sure."

"They left instructions for me to select people from the village who are well experienced musicians, and I can think of no one better than you three. If Ray and Megan had not wanted any of you, they would have told me. So if you are all willing to serve please sign these forms." He pushed some papers across the table.

Dr. Morgan responded gruffly,

"Well everyone knows that Bryn and I didn't get on with the man when he was alive, to put it mildly, but we'll both do the best we can for him now he's dead. Yes, Bryn?"

"Yes. Handel. That's the least we can do."

"Oh. I am so glad, Bryn." Phoebe whispered, "I was afraid you might refuse."

"Well that's settled then," broke in the solicitor, "That's right. Just sign there and I'll witness your signatures. Now, there's one important thing you need to decide: who is going to be the recipient of the first grant?"

The three new Trustees looked at each other, and immediately Phoebe said,

"I imagine that's obvious to us all."

"Yes," responded Bryn and the doctor in unison,

"Ron Thomas should be the first," continued the doctor. Bryn nodded, and turning to the solicitor, he added,

"I think we're all agreed on that." Ron Thomas whom they had selected, was the son of Karen, and a brilliant young pianist studying at the local school.

"He's not too young though, is he? He won't be ready for college for a year or two," interjected Phoebe, looking concerned.

"The Trust deeds say nothing about age, just that the money should be used for the candidate's musical education. We all know the struggle Karen has had bringing Ron up on her own. I would think it totally appropriate for us to support the rest of his schooling before he goes on to college, if he's the one you've selected. But it's your decision," added Mr. Evans, formally.

"Sounds sensible to me," confirmed Bryn, and the doctor nodded his assent.

"That's it then, we're agreed. Who'll tell Karen and Ron?"

"I'd quite like to do that, if it's all right with you two?" Queried Phoebe.

"That's fine." Said the doctor.

"Yes. You do it Phoebe, you're probably closer to Karen than us three." Bryn smiled at her, "You know, I think I'm beginning to change my opinion of Ray Roberts."

"I'm so glad to hear that, Bryn, it'll be a weight off your shoulders. You can't do much now about all the quarrelling you two did while he was alive, but at least

*Strange Harmony*

you can reconcile yourself to his memory. Hanging on to grudges never helped anybody."

Bryn looked at her quizzically, but the moment passed as she left the room.

# *Chapter 26*
# Maggie's Baby

After the meeting with the solicitor, Phoebe went straight to tell Karen the good news. Karen was sitting in her café and grocery store on her own so Phoebe went to sit by her

"Karen," she said "Are you sitting comfortably? I've got some wonderful news for you."

"Thank goodness for that. With Dad going back to prison again I need a bit of a lift."

"Well this will give you a big lift: Megan and Ray Roberts have put their whole estate into a Trust Fund."

"Yes . . . .?"

"It's for musically gifted children of the village, and your Ron has been given the first grant from it."

"WHAT? MY RON? That's wonderful! He was going to go down the mine with all the other lads at the end of this year . . . ."

"Well now he'll be able to go to college like you wanted him to. There's plenty enough money in the grant to see him through to a degree in music, if that's what he wants."

"He's always wanted to be a concert pianist really, but I don't know that he's that good. The Trust is Roberts' money, you say?"

"That's right. They were always interested in music, as you know, and with no children of their own, they wanted to help other peoples' children I suppose."

Karen looked at her friend with amazement.

"Phoebe? Can you keep a really close secret?" She asked.

"Of course I can. What is it?"

"It's almost laughable, if it hadn't been so awful when it happened, but Ron is actually Ray Robert's son; he seduced me fifteen years ago and Ron was the result. I never told anyone who the father was, and I wouldn't let Ray give me any help because then I was very angry and very proud. Now he's going to pay for Ron's education through his Trust fund. I don't know whether to laugh or cry. But it must still remain a secret."

"Well to tell you the truth, when I heard you were pregnant all those years ago, I had my suspicions that Ray Roberts might have been responsible: you were a very attractive girl and he was always a womaniser."

"Even up to the time he died," said Karen.

"I promise I won't say a word to anyone about you and Ray."

"Thanks, Phoebe. I know you'll keep my secret. The other funny thing about all this is that Megan Roberts gave Ron piano lessons when he was younger and would never let me pay her for them. I wonder if Ray had told her? It was she who started Ron off on his music really; she reckoned he would be very good. Amazing how these things work out, isn't it?"

"Karen?" Phoebe asked her friend, "You implied just then that Ray Roberts was still a womaniser? Surely he's not the one responsible for . . . .?"

"For Maggie's baby as well? I'm afraid he is. You know she's been working up at his house . . ."

"But he was her uncle! I thought it was one of the boys at school got her pregnant."

"No. She's certain it was Ray. Don't worry he wasn't her real uncle so the baby should be all right."

"The baby may be, but I don't think Maggie is. She's been coming to see me since her father shut her out of his house, and she's been getting more and more listless as the pregnancy has gone on. I didn't like the look of her at all, the last time I saw her and she's nearly due. But you must have noticed how she's gone down hill since she's been staying with you."

"Yes, I suppose so, but I just put it down to the way her father acted when he found out she was pregnant. She got very upset about him, though she must have known what he was like."

*Strange Harmony*

"I thought it was a terrible thing to do, though I suppose it was no worse than what other fathers have done in the past."

"It makes you wonder if they had any love for their daughters at all. I can't understand them," answered Karen, shaking her head as she remembered how her own father had forgiven her when she had become pregnant as a young girl and had refused to say who the father was.

Suddenly, as they were talking, Bryn burst into the café, and blurted out, breathlessly,

"Phoebe. There you are! I've been looking for you everywhere. Dr. Handel wants you to help him. Urgently. Up at the hospital. It's Maggie!

"Oh, no," responded Phoebe. "I knew she'd have trouble. Will you two come as well?"

Karen quickly put a closed notice on the door of the café and the three anxious friends ran out of the village to the little hospital nearby. Phoebe walked quietly into the tiny labour ward where Dr. Handel Morgan was bending over his patient.

"Maggie came to the surgery this morning in some distress," said the doctor,

"I brought her straight in here and sent for you. So glad to see you. She's had the baby. Can you see to him, nurse please." Dr. Morgan assumed his formal medical role, and Phoebe responded by checking the baby.

"He's big, isn't he. But he looks fine, doctor."

"Thank goodness. We've got problems here though, nurse. I can't stop the bleeding, and she's unconscious. Could you come and help with this padding?"

Phoebe handed the baby to an ashen-faced helper who had been watching the drama as it unfolded in the ward, and moved to assist the doctor in her quiet, efficient way.

"I've seen this before, I am afraid," she said, looking at Maggie professionally.

"Yes. So have I." They had shared in many births before, most of them straight forward and successful, but some difficult and dangerous: they knew only too well the usually inevitable consequences of the mother haemorrhaging excessively after the birth.

They worked together for a while over the girl, then the doctor straightened up and said,

"Well, we can't do anymore for her. She was just very unlucky, poor girl."

Phoebe, her eyes streaming with tears, stared at the still, pale figure lying on the white, blood-stained sheets.

"Oh, I am sorry," she sobbed, "Maggie was always so alive. It's awful to see her like this."

"Well, we did our best. It's just one of those things." The doctor sighed.

Phoebe wiped her tears and took the baby from the helper to cradle him in her arms.

"And what'll happen to this little thing now, I wonder?. Yet another orphan for the village to find a home for,

*Strange Harmony*

Maggie's father certainly won't want to have anything to do with him."

By this time Bryn and Karen, having heard from the waiting room what had been going on in the labour ward, joined the tragic tableau that had formed there. Bryn found himself considerably affected by being present at Maggie's death: he had become very fond of the girl as he had helped her improve her singing. His heart pounded as he looked at the tiny figure of Phoebe, her face still damp from her tears, holding the baby and gazing at it with such obvious concern and love.

Then his heart momentarily faltered, as Phoebe turned to look straight at him and said quietly with peculiar warmth,

"Bryn, do you think . . . .?"

"Yes. Phoebe, I'm thinking the same as you. *We* could look after him."

"We'd have to . . . ."

"Yes, my love, we'd have to get married first and adopt him properly."

Dr. Morgan and Karen and the ward helper looked on in a mixture of delight and shock as Bryn put his arms around the little woman holding the baby so gently.

"But Bryn . . . . ?" The doctor started to ask. Bryn butted in,

"It's all right Handel, and you Karen. You don't need to look so surprised. We've been thinking of getting married for a while now. We just needed the right opportunity—and this is obviously it."

"Not really surprised, just absolutely delighted. You're made for each other!" Answered the doctor, shaking Bryn's free hand vigorously.

Phoebe looked up at Bryn with her eyes shining, clearly agreeing with the doctor's sentiments. Karen moved over to hug her friend, and said

"Oh, Phoebe. I'm so glad for you. Maggie would have been too."

Phoebe looked down at the dead girl, put the baby briefly on her cold arm and said brokenly, with a smile,

"It's all right Maggie . . . . we'll love him . . . . and . . . . look after him for you. You just rest in peace."

The line from his favourite choir piece sounded in Bryn's head and warmed his heart '. . . . sweet peace sits crowned with smiles . . . .' it sang. It immediately reminded him of what was ahead of them, and he laughed out loud at the emotion of the moment as he addressed his wife-to-be,

"We wouldn't want to call him Ray, would we? But he could be Robert, kind of in memory of both the Roberts, seeing they gave their money to the Trust. You never know, maybe he'll benefit from it one day too."

"Yes, I think Bob Griffiths sounds fine," replied Phoebe, grateful to hear that Bryn seemed to be thinking much more positively about Ray and Megan.

*Strange Harmony*

"But the wedding will have to wait, my love," he warned her, with a smile,

"Remember, we've got the international concert in the Albert Hall next month. Let's get that over with first, then we can concentrate on getting married. We'll make it the event of the year and involve the whole village."

# Chapter 27
# The Concert

The train journey to London passed uneventfully. The whole choir bubbled with excitement, some of them busily and nervously talking all the way, remarking enthusiastically on practically everything they saw: the greenness of the fields, the apples in the orchards and the size of the houses. The colour and sparkle of the rivers struck them particularly as they had only ever seen the coal black rivers of South Wales. The darkness of the Severn tunnel quietened some of them down for a while, but they were soon chatting away excitedly again. Many of them had not even been as far as Cardiff before, let alone London, and, for quite a few of them, this was their first train journey. The thought of going to the capital city of England filled them with a mixture of trepidation and anticipation.

Even more, performing at the Albert Hall was totally beyond their imagination. But it soon was to become a reality for all of them.

They had changed at their nearby London hotel, another first for them, and paid for, like their train travel, by the concert organisers. So now they stood inside the

Albert Hall. Waiting their turn to perform. They all looked very professional, even if they didn't exactly feel it, in their uniforms of blue and black, the men in their freshly pressed blazers, a small red rose in each man's lapel, and the women in their smart, black dresses, also displaying a red rose. Bryn had said that the roses were for luck; not that they really needed any, for they were so well practised by this time, they were close to perfection, as he had told them proudly.

The huge dome of the magnificent auditorium astonished them. They had never seen, or performed in a hall any where near its size before. The galleries of seats rose up like terracing around them, dwarfing them all. They stared back at the thousands of faces looking expectantly down on them. They were aware of the pipes of the great organ which acted as a seried back-drop behind them. On one side of the enormous stage stood a gleaming, black Bluthner grand piano, waiting patiently for Phoebe's fingers to caress it.

A number of choirs from other countries had performed before them on the programme, all especially selected for their excellence. One from Africa and another from Austria had been particularly well received. Now it was their turn. They had never been so excited. Nervousness threatened to overcome them. A hushed murmur ran around the international audience. It was the first time most of them would have heard a Welsh choir.

Bryn took his place in front of the choir, standing tall, his back straight and his head held high. This immediately hushed the immense audience. He could feel the silence. He touched the red rose in his lapel that his Phoebe had given him. It was not for luck, she had said, but for love. He looked around the choir and gave them his usual confident smile. He willed them to perform at their very best. This, he felt was his chance. This is what he had been living and working for. This was the moment to cement his reputation as one of the leading conductors in Great Britain.

He raised his baton with a slight flourish and nodded to Phoebe, who played a quiet chord of E minor. They had decided to sing Parry's 'My Soul', the piece that had won them their very first competition just after the mine explosion which had devastated their village, a fact that the organiser's had seen fit to include in the write-up about them in the programme, because of its human interest to the London audience.

Bryn mouthed the words 'My Soul,' with the choir as they came in as one with the familiar opening chords. He was immediately transported by the music. He was in his element. This is what he was meant to do. Made to do, he thought briefly, as like the whole choir, he was carried onwards and upwards by the magnificence of the music. He was not to know until later, but in that moment the whole audience too, was caught up in the intensity of the experience, and their positive reactions communicated themselves back to the members of the choir, who responded by expressing even more powerfully the depth of feeling the piece always stimulated in them.

Bryn knew the choir had never sung like this before. The challenge and the importance of the occasion had clearly affected every singer, and they had responded with more than their usual confidence and fervour. He experienced again, as he had when they first sang the now familiar piece, a strange feeling of wholeness. He was at one with the choir and the music, totally united with them: an amazing feeling of contentment.

At that point, the choir sang '. . . . the Rose that cannot wither, Thy fortress and thy ease . . . .' Fortress! That was it. He felt, in all the surrounding insecurity of an international performance in the Albert Hall, London, as though he was residing in a secure fortress—totally at ease. At ease with himself, at ease with their performance, at ease with the world. And the music had done it for him. He felt he had caught an echo of that strange harmony that Phoebe had tried to describe for him: the harmony that comes from the soul of the universe, which he had first heard when he entered that rescue cage.

The singers were now into the final section: the part that, musically, in the key of G major, always satisfied him the most, but at the same time, intellectually, totally mystified him, '. . . . None can thee secure but One who never changes . . . .' One who never changes? There could not possibly *be* such a thing, at least, he had neither the experience or the words for it. But then the choir burst into the final chords of their performance, and in their song, found the words for him 'Thy God', they sang, 'Thy Life, Thy Cure'.

And suddenly, in an amazing revelation, just as the audience exploded in thunderous applause, he realised what Phoebe had been trying to teach him ever since he had known her. And to crown the experience, the people in the audience started to stand as they applauded, first in their tens and then in hundreds. He looked around the choir and smiled to find many of them with tears in their eyes, absorbing the enthusiastic adulation with a mixture of relief and delight. He watched proudly as one of the organisers walked up to Phoebe at the piano and presented her with an immense bouquet. Fortunately, they were roses in a red that exactly matched the colour of the roses the choir had worn throughout their performance. It formed a beautiful picture that he felt would remain with him for ever.

'. . . . The Rose that cannot wither . . . .' thought Bryn. But then the faces of his friend Bill, and all the other miners in that rescue cage came to mind, as they always did when his emotions got the better of him.

His hand went up to the rose in his lapel, and he thought with great sadness, that that rose would wither, as

Bill had withered and died under that rock-fall, and as he himself would one day wither, and Phoebe too. But as he looked at his accompanist, he also knew that the love they had found together through their music, the love that they would now share with little Robert, *that* was the rose that would never wither. And it was theirs to keep and treasure.